The Abandoned Prince

Table of Contents

i. **Playlist** – Page 3
ii. **Author's Warning** – Page 4
iii. **Preface** – Page 5
iv. **Chapter 1 – Klaus Malik** – Page 8
v. **Chapter 2 – Klaus** – Page 23
vi. **Chapter 3 – Klaus** – Page 31
vii. **Chapter 4 – Claudianne Jakard** – Page 42
viii. **Chapter 5 – Claudianne** – Page 59
ix. **Chapter 6 – Klaus** – Page 71
x. **Chapter 7 – Klaus** – Page 84
xi. **Chapter 8 – Claudianne** – Page 96
xii. **Chapter 9 – Klaus** – Page 106
xiii. **Chapter 10 – Claudianne** – Page 117
xiv. **Chapter 11 – Claudianne** – Page 126
xv. **Chapter 12 – Klaus** – Page 137
xvi. **Chapter 13 – Klaus** – Page 149
xvii. **Chapter 14 – Claudianne** – Page 160
xviii. **Chapter 15 – Klaus Malik Jakard** – Page 172
xix. **Chapter 16 – Claudianne** – Page 182
xx. **Chapter 17 – Klaus** – Page 194
xxi. **Chapter 18 – Claudianne & Klaus** – Page 205
xxii. **Chapter 19 – Klaus** – Page 216
xxiii. **Epilogue – Claudianne** – Page 231
xxiv. **Bonus Chapter 1 – Kaleem Jakard** – Page 233
xxv. **Bonus Chapter 2 – Cavell Jakard Luther** – Page 236
xxvi. **Bonus Chapter 3 – Kadi Jakard Ali** – Page 244
xxvii. **Extras** – Page 249
xxviii. **Book 7 Excerpt: Celine** – Page 252
xxix. **Books by Kristen Elizabeth** – Page 257
xxx. **Acknowledgments** – Page 260
xxxi. **About the Author** – Page 261

The Royal's Saga, Book 6: The Abandoned Prince

Book 6 Theme: Chariot Race – Various Artists – Selections from the Prince of Egypt soundtrack

Muse Playlist (Alphabetical Order)

1. Ancient Egyptian Music – Bastet
2. Ancient Egyptian Music – Pharoah Ramses II
3. Apocalyptica ft. Brent Smith – Not Strong Enough
4. Asaya (Original Remix)
5. Breaking Benjamin – The Dark of You
6. Citizen Soldier – Death of Me
7. Clean Bandit ft. Sean Paul & Anne-Marie – Rockabye
8. CLAUDIANNE theme: Meditation Music Zone – White Lotus Flower
9. Dark Egyptian Music – Anubis
10. Doja Cat – Woman
11. Elley Duhe – Middle of the Night (Slowed & Reverb version)
12. Epic Egyptian Music – Apophis
13. KLAUS theme: Smashtrax – Prince of Persian
14. Maneskin – Beggin
15. Monoir & Dharia – Incredible (Slowed & Reverb version)
16. Rex Mundi ft. Susana – Nothing at All
17. Sam Tinnesz – Play with Fire (Slowed & Reverb version)
18. Separate Ways – Journey
19. Skrillex & Damian Jr. Gong Marley – Make it Bun Dem
20. Spice, Sean Paul & Shaggy – Go Down Deh
21. The Arabian Night – Instrumental Belly Dance music

Author's Warning:

This book contains trigger warnings and material, including:

Bullying
Assault/gore
Attempted Kidnapping
Witch Craft
Attempted Murder/Murder
Drugging/bondage/rape
Miscarriage

These triggers can be found in the following chapters:
Preface, Chapters 7, **8**, 9, **10**, **11**, **12**, **14**, 15
(*chapters with hard triggers*)

Please proceed with caution, and if triggered by any of these themes or by the story, please seek the appropriate help or resources. Be safe! Thank you!

Preface

September, 139 Imperial year

"Stop that thief!" The stand-owner shouted as I bolted, a sack of gold in my hand as I ran.

I chuckled, knowing that there was no way that they would catch up.

None of the soldiers in this country could ever keep up with me.

I stuck out, certainly; I was dark-skinned, well-tanned with ashen-gray hair, and bright, vivid purple eyes.

It was hard not to notice me.

Most of the people in this country were the same skin tone as I, yes, but most had black or dark brown hair and dark eyes.

I struck down an alley, when I ran full-forced into a situation I hadn't expected, and despite my current situation…I just couldn't ignore.

A young, pale-in-comparison to me, silver-haired girl cornered by a group of masked boys who only looked a little older than she was, by their size.

She, herself, looked to be about twelve, if I had to guess, and she had bright purple eyes…

Purple eyes...? The same as me...?

Were we related, somehow?

I had to know who she was!

I had been desperately searching for my origins, at my guardian's urging.

"Get away!" She cried, trying to get away, but the leader at the center grabbed her and shoved her against the wall.

"Let her go!" I said, dropping my sack of coins and rushing over, shoving my full weight into the leader.

He stumbled back, practically snarling as he grabbed a dagger from his belt. "Did you just shove me, boy?" He asked.

I smirked. "I don't see anyone else here. How about you pick on someone your own size, and leave the little girl alone?"

He glanced at my discarded sack of gold. "You're nothing but a petty thief yourself! Do you even know who this girl *is*? She's the daughter of the Archduke!" He gestured to her. "She is next in line to the *throne*. If we ransomed her, we'd get enough gold to last a *lifetime*. Why don't you use your brain for a minute and join *us*, instead?"

I rolled my eyes. "Yeah, sure, I'll just do that," I scoffed, sputtering out my tongue and blowing a raspberry before I gave a thumbs-down. "No, thanks," I said, and I shot my hand forward, snatching the blade from his grip. "Sorry, I don't like taking advantage of little girls. Sounds like a rather perverse habit."

He gaped at me. "H-how?!" He cried while the girl insisted she wasn't a little girl.

That was cute...

"There they are!" I heard the guards shouting, but I was too preoccupied to think much on it...

That was, until I was *rudely* tackled to the ground.

Well...

Fuck.

*Just...**fuck**.*

Chapter 1 – Klaus Malik

July, 139 Imperial year

"How was the bazaar today?" My guardian asked, and I glanced at him as he reverted back to his human form from his cat form.

The mighty sorcerer, Qassim Malik, had found me as an infant and had raised me as his own.

With his dark, russet-bronze skin and pure silver hair, and his medium-toned gray eyes…his identity as a sorcerer was quite clear.

Only sorcerers had silver hair and light-colored eyes.

He had told me, when I had turned ten, that I was not actually of his bloodline…that he was my adoptive parent.

My siblings hadn't been surprised, but I had been, and it humbled me to know that they had always treated me as family, regardless.

If anything, they were a little too good to me, sometimes. I was rather spoiled, really.

Lately, however, since I had turned thirteen just over a year ago, things had started to change…

I brushed my silvery, peppery grey hair out of my bright, vivid, light purple eyes.

He had been pushing me to listen to rumors about the palace for him, as he wanted to stay informed.

He also wanted me to start digging into my roots, as my journey as a powerful sorcerer would require some basic knowledge of my familial background to some extent, but also because my mana was blocked by the fact that I had no connection to my roots.

Being connected to your roots and knowing about your background and who you are was extremely important to unlocking your mana and becoming—and surviving—the coming of age as an adult with mana.

As a mage, if you came of age without being connected to your roots...your mana would mutate and transform inside of you to become poison, and you would eventually suffer from mana implosion—you would blow up from the inside.

It was gory, disgusting, and said to be horrendously painful.

"I suppose it was alright, but I didn't learn much," I admitted. "The only thing that I heard today was more of the same rumors we've already heard lately; the princess is being prepped for marriage." I sighed, shaking my head. "It seems a bit excessive, she's only, what...twelve?"

He sighed, and stroked his chin before he started pacing. "Yes...far too young to be worrying about marrying a stranger for the throne. If only she could become the ruler without that, but even then, I don't feel that she'd be out of danger."

I hesitated, not really knowing what to say.

Every time that I asked Qassim about the throne, or the royal family, he shut down.

He wouldn't discuss it with me beyond the basic histories, but even then, he didn't go into bloodlines or the reason for the…regicides.

According to my adoptive father, he had once been the predominant palace sorcerer, working directly under the sultan and his sultana as their chief advisor and closest friend. Now, he was just a regular marquis-ranked civilian sorcerer.

From what I had learned about the histories, there had been three children of the sultan: two sons, and one daughter. The eldest son rose to become sultan.

My adopted father had been a sorcerer for this sultan, and according to his firsthand recounting of it…it had been deep into the night, one night, when there had been a scream in the night, and the entire palace had gone into an upheaval as the bodies of the sultan, sultana, the favored imperial concubine, the first prince, second prince, princess, and even the *concubine's* daughter—the youngest princess—had all been murdered.

Radicals conspiring against the throne, against the sultan and sultana and their children—a family that were openly mages—had come in and done away with them all.

To this day, the conspirators inside of the palace were still unidentified.

The sultan's younger brother—the middle child of the family—had taken over rule for a short while…until he and his wife had been murdered during the night just before he had even formally taken up the mantle of Sultan and Sultana at all. They hadn't even had children, yet, as he had only been seventeen at the time.

As a result of that horrible night, the rule of the nation had been up in the air, but with the help of allied kingdoms and empires, we had managed to survive.

Now, with the rule shifting to the family of the Archduke, the deceased Sultan and deceased almost-sultan's younger brother-in-law, the nation was beginning to thrive and find order again.

There was only one problem...

The Archduke and his Archduchess, Faiza Jakard—the deceased sultans' youngest sibling, the former princess—had not had any sons. They had a single daughter who had only turned twelve this year; Claudianne Jakard.

Now, the Archduchess was gravely ill, and there was no way that the kingdom could last until the Archduke remarried and had a son. Claudianne was the only one capable of taking on the role of ruling the nation.

This put them, as the last family of the imperial bloodline, at a disadvantage. No woman had ever become the ruler on her own. This put tremendous pressure on the Archduke and Archduchess to marry their daughter to a reputable lord, and quickly, since the Archduke would likely be a widower, soon.

"I am glad, at least, that the princess has Amir," he said. "Amir is one of the most competent soldiers in the palace, and he was absolutely loyal to the royal family. She should be safe, if she sticks close to him, but if I remember right, he was a bit of a...difficult man. Uncompromising and cold."

Sometimes, it was odd to hear him talk about people in the palace like he was so aware of them. It reminded me that he had, at one time, worked in the palace.

"Father?" I asked, and he gave me his attention. "Do you...use your cat form to go to the palace?"

He hesitated, before he laughed. "I suppose there is no hiding it." He sighed. "I do go, in my feline form, to explore and catch wind of rumors. I haven't been back in my human form since the night I resigned—the day after the...darkest night," he said, a faraway expression on his face. "Have you managed to perform the shift yet?" He asked.

I shook my head. "Not quite," I said. "I manage to get part of the way through the shift, but then the magic reverses. I'm not sure what's going wrong with it."

"Hm...are you sure you're pulling enough power? Are you pulling the mana to your belly, as I showed you?"

I knew that I didn't have much mana to work with, because I hadn't attached to my roots yet, but I should still be able to pull off a minor shift into a small animal like that.

"Well, it is a bit hard for me to feel it. I pull and pull, reaching for the strings of my mana, but I barely feel them...I feel like I'm reaching through them, rather than touching them."

His eyes widened. "Oh...oh, dear," he said, faltering a bit and plopping down into his chair in the sitting room. "That isn't good."

"What does that mean?" I asked.

He met my eyes. "You must uncover your roots, Klaus. Your mana streams are thinning faster than I had anticipated. At this rate, the implosion will happen sooner rather than later...or, the opposite will happen—you will just lose your mana and drain out your vitality that way. Either way is horrible."

I threw my hands in the air, exasperated. "What do you want from me? Do you think I haven't tried? You won't even give me clues! I don't even know what it is that I am looking for! Can't you just...tell me?"

"I *cannot*," he said, firm. "There are things that I have hinted at before, and you have never realized...perhaps you should think back to our previous conversations and try to put the pieces together," he told me. "The only thing that I can openly admit to you...is that you are not of my blood, you were always loved, you have special magic capabilities that are unique, and you were named for one of your ancestors. However, above all else...if you do not figure out your true identity and return to the source of your mana streams, and get solidified in your power...you will die."

Then, before I could respond and before he said anything else, he stood and left the room, leaving me sputtering and gaping after him.

I sighed, trying to come to terms with my thoughts.

"'Think back to our previous conversations and try to put the pieces together'," I recited softly.

I tried hard to think back on all of our recent conversations.

Only a few stuck out to me.

He had been working me to the bone, trying to show me the shifting magic, specifically so that I could travel "safely."

He had put so much drastic, almost dramatic emphasis on the word "safely," that it had struck me as a little odd...he had sounded borderline paranoid. He hadn't ever liked for me to travel around without some kind of disguise, or spell to hide my features, that was true enough.

He had never wanted me to travel around outside of the home without concealing my appearance.

To stick out so oddly, though, for him to focus so hard on "safety" …what did I need to stay so safe from?

Then, there were my mana qualities. He said that my magic capabilities were *unique*, and that I had special mana, which meant that my mana flow was different than other mage families…at least, in this country.

Several nations had mages, so could it be that I, perhaps, didn't originally belong to this nation at all, or that one of my ancestors belonged to a different nation?

Adding on to the top of that, of course, being that I was adopted, my blood was not of my adoptive father's…but it did beg the question; If I hadn't been even a distant relative, how *had* he found me in the first place? Had he found me on the streets?

He had always told me that he'd found me and took me in, and yet, he had admitted just now that I had always been loved…and he had said it with such conviction that it led me to believe that he did, in fact, know who my parents were. *Wait…*

He had just said that I was *named after* one of my ancestors, but if that were the case…then, if he had simply found me and taken me in, he wouldn't even know who my ancestors were, would he? That meant that the possibility of him finding me out on the streets was out, too.

So, let me piece this together.

One, I had mana that was unusual and didn't match other mana types in the area because I hadn't found my mana roots yet, and I had been all over the kingdom.

Two, I had to be sure to do everything with as much caution for my safety as possible, because it was dangerous for me to be identified, for some reason.

Three, he wasn't related to me in our bloodlines, so I wasn't family. He had not adopted me from a relative…

Four, I hadn't been found on the streets at random, which meant that Qassim had, somehow, known my family.

Five, he not only knew who my family and my ancestors were, but also that I was named after one of them.

So, on that last point specifically; Klaus wasn't exactly a *common* name in this country…

There were only a couple of families in this area that held uncommon names such as that, and all of them had foreign blood in their backgrounds.

Wait…wait, wait, wait a minute.

Was I foreign?

I knew, though, that this thought wouldn't have made any sense at all. I had never seen him meeting with foreigners, either. Qassim was rather shut in and solitary, and spent most of his days working in his laboratory.

I also knew well enough that Qassim hadn't ever been out of this country.

He had told me so before, when I had asked him about his adventures when I was a child. I was very interested in travel, and adventures, and treasure hunting when I was growing up…

I had asked him, as a result, if he had ever been outside of the country, and he had admitted that he *hadn't*. I knew for a fact that he hadn't left the country just since I had asked that question, either.

None of this made any sense at all to me, but I was expected and forced to figure this out on my own?

My head hurt, and I felt my mana streams thinning even more.

If I didn't find the root of my mana and solidify my mana streams, I would die...

There weren't many mages that had *this* issue, in particular, because most mages knew their roots. Most of them already had that connection. The fact that I was a mage, a high commodity in this part of the world, was another clue, more rather.

The fact that he *couldn't* tell me was yet another clue, but *why* couldn't he tell me himself? Was there a spell with that condition...?

Trying to figure this out on my own was far too strenuous.

Every time that I thought that I was getting close to piecing it together, figuring it all out...then, there were things that didn't make sense.

Whenever that happened, there were sharp, stabbing pains in my head.

Why was I in pain when I was only trying to figure out my origins...? It didn't make sense.

I continued wracking my brain through the waves of stabbing pain, trying to think of anything else that may have stuck out to me—

Wait...

Wait, he had wanted me to pay attention to the imperial family, hadn't he?

Then, that could be a clue...or, out of his devotion to the sultan.

He had, after all, once been the most trusted advisor and sorcerer to the sultan and his sultana, so he could just be showing favor and patriotism for his rulers and trying to look out for their last living relatives.

Which brought my attention back to that issue.

The princess was supposed to be, at this point in time, undergoing preparations for marriage. She was the only child Archduke Balin Habim, a cousin of the original Sultan, who had married the Sultan's youngest sister, Faiza Jakard.

Now that they were taking over the ruling of the country, their surname was turning to the youngest sister's original maiden surname, Jakard, in order to keep the name of the original imperial line going.

Any husband that married the princess would be taking her surname, as well.

I rolled over all of this in my mind.

I would need to do some more digging.

September, 139 IY

Fuck.

Just...*fuck*.

I had only been trying to make off with something that my adoptive father needed.

For it wasn't just gold in the sack in my hand—it had been, rather, the shining and sparkling amethyst in the sack that had caught my eye as the nobleman had been digging into it, and my father had told me that I needed amethyst to help strengthen my connection to my mana, to help me into the cat shift without drawing out more of my own power.

Each sorcerer had a particular stone that matched their mana, and amplified it without sucking away their mana directly.

This item could possibly help me immensely.

The gold had just been an added bonus.

I admit, I shouldn't have stolen it, but Qassim didn't make much money anymore, and he didn't have any on hand.

I was going to pay it back, honest.

Then, I had only tried to do something good by rescuing the young girl who had been being kidnapped.

I tried to lift my face from the ground, but the guards held me in place, snapping the bag out of my hands.

I sighed.

"Claudianne? Claud, where—oh, heavens!" A male voice called, rushing over and pulling the girl into his arms. "What's going on? What happened?" He demanded. His eyes flew to me. "Did this boy hurt you?"

"No, papa, I—"

"I'll see him hanged for daring to touch the princess of this kingdom, and I—"

"He didn't hurt me!" The girl shouted, stomping her foot and pulling away from him before she rushed to my side. She shooed the guards back, who glanced at one another but didn't move.

"You dare intercede my daughter? The princess Claudianne Jakard?" The man asked. "I am Archduke Jakard, currently ruling over the Jakard kingdom," he scowled at them, and they finally let me go and moved out of the girl's way.

"But sire, the boy is a thief—"

"He saved my life, papa!" The girl said, resolute. "He...he found the men who were kidnapping me...! The group of grown men! And he took them on, all by himself! He could have been killed, but he stood up for me even before he knew who I was. Papa, I want him for my personal guard."

The city guards openly gaped at us, and took in the scene around them.

One had been caught down the alleyway, while the rest had been fleeing the scene.

That man was dragged over, and the princess pointed at him. "They knew who I was. They dragged me away from the bazaar and my guards, papa, and told me they'd cut out my tongue if I didn't keep silent! Then, they were going to ransom me! They told this boy, when he tried to stop them, that he should join them and he said no and even managed to disarm one! Papa, please…father, I humbly implore you, allow me to have him as my guard. He is more competent and braver than my other guards."

Her other guards, who had come with her father, backed away a bit, even as her father glanced at me.

"Help him up, and let's have a look at him then," he said, and she motioned for the guards to help me to my feet. "Look at me, boy," he told me.

I looked up, meeting his eyes, and his eyes shot wide and gaped at me for a moment before they narrowed and he looked me up and down as he "hm'd."

He did not look much like his daughter at all. He had dark, raven black hair, and golden-hazel eyes, and a considerable-sized build. He wore rich, high-quality clothing.

"You are a mage?"

I startled a bit, and looked down to see that the glass of my pendant that had been containing my disguise talisman had shattered, the talisman gone. Obviously from being tackled to the ground.

My true appearance was visible, rather than my cover.

Double "**fuck**."

I sighed, and hesitantly nodded. Because my disguising talisman was gone and I no longer held a normal appearance, it was useless to try to lie. "Yes, sir."

"...You are a thief?"

I looked away. "I was seeking the stone inside, only, to help solidify my mana. I didn't have the gold to afford the stone. I planned to return the gold, later."

The man motioned for the bag, and the guard nearest him handed it to him. He fiddled inside for a moment before he pulled out the amethyst, and his eyes met mine sharply.

"...Your Mana Stone is *Amethyst*?" He asked, tone hard.

I nodded. "Y-yes," I answered, not sure how that was relevant. Did that upset him...?

He looked me up and down again. Then, he looked to his daughter again before he looked back to me. "...Are you willing to serve my daughter, as her personal guard?"

I glanced at her, with her bright and hopeful purple eyes that were darker than mine but still just as rich.

I met his eyes again and nodded. "I am willing to do my best."

He looked to her, then. "He is your responsibility. You will see to his living arrangements, his food, his training...everything. You will be the Sultana, once you marry, and this will be a good chance to give you some authority and responsibility to see how well you handle being in charge of people." He threw one more glance at me, before he turned, and began to walk away.

The girl rushed over to me, smiling brightly. "Come, come! I will take you back to the palace with me and show you where you'll be staying."

"W-wait, I—"

"Come, you'll love the palace! I'll be sure that you are well taken care of!" She said, not listening in the slightest.

With no further protest, I followed her a bit hesitantly.

Would Qassim worry about me too much before I got a chance to reach out to him and let him know what had happened...?

Chapter 2 – Klaus

"I will give you the chambers beside of mine," she told me, hands on her hips proudly. "They are good chambers. You should find all the amenities you need inside. My other guard, Amir, stays in the chambers across the hall, there," she said, gesturing at the door. "Also," she said, having me follow her into her chambers. There stood several handmaidens. "One of these maidens will be serving you, and will help you adjust to life here. Ah, Amir!" She grinned brightly, and I turned to see a man step into the room.

He looked to be in his mid to late thirties or so.

He had dark brown hair, bright golden eyes, and rich dark skin. He was also very well-built, and I could tell that he had spent most of his life training.

He wore a head-guard's uniform, and there was a deep scar over his right eye that cut from the jaw, all the way up into the hairline. The iris of his right eye was slightly lighter than his left, meaning there had been a bit of damage to the eye.

"This is my new personal guard, um…" She glanced to me. "I feel so bad for not asking sooner, but…what is your name?"

"Klaus Malik, your highness," I told her, and the guard stiffened a bit.

I fidgeted a bit under his powerful scrutiny.

Why was he staring at me so intensely...?

"This is my new personal guard, Klaus Malik," the princess beamed at us, oblivious to the mood shift in the room. "He saved me from *kidnappers* today, and tried to take on the group by himself. He was so *brave*," she said, smiling at me warmly.

Amir, who was known throughout the kingdom as being cold, certainly proved why he had that reputation when he glared at me. "That certainly is brave of him, your highness. I am glad you are safe. I should have been there, rather than the young guards, and then he wouldn't have had to intervene."

Something about his tone made me feel like he looked down on me...

"You will be training him from this point forward," she told him.

"*What*? But, princess, I—"

"Ah, ah, ah," she said, wagging her fingers in a "no" gesture. "*Who* is the princess, here?"

He sighed, and took a knee. "Yes, your highness," he said. "As you command it."

"Try not to sound so disheartened! Look, he has skill! He has mana, and he's really fast! It should be no problem, and I'm sure he will learn fast! Please, Amir. I hope you will be kind to him. Well," she said, looking at the window and at the darkening sky outside. "It should be around supper time, now. I will direct the maids to bring your meal to your chambers so that you can settle in, and you can begin your training in the morning, yes?" She asked me, and I nodded.

"Yes, your highness," me and Amir echoed, and he glanced at me. "Be ready at sunrise. If you are late, don't bother showing up at all," he said, before he turned and walked back across the hall and shut his door behind him with a hard thud.

"Ignore him," the princess laughed…and then, she did something I did not expect—she threw her arms around me in a hug.

I almost lost all the breath in my lungs as warmth and soothing, gentle pressure filled me…

The stark difference was so startling that she, herself, noticed it. She backed up.

"Klaus?" She asked. "Are you okay?"

I cleared my throat. "I'm sorry, princess, I'm not used to hugs," I said, smiling at her. "Thank you for that. Can we…try another?" I asked, holding my arms open.

She gave me a sad, sympathetic expression for a moment before she beamed at me. "Sure!" She said too brightly, too innocently…and then she pressed me into another hug.

My heart almost skipped a beat, and I felt my mana streams strengthening and thickening a little more. I felt breathless from the added weight of comfort. For the first time…I did not feel empty.

Oh, heavens above…

*This girl…**she** had something to do with my mana roots, I knew it! …Though…what?*

When I had seen her silver hair and purple eyes, I had thought it was odd that we would share that same particular combination.

Purple eyes were not a mage trait in themselves. The silver hair, yes, but not the purple eyes.

She was some part of me, but *what…?*

None of this made any sense.

"I just wanted to say thank you, for saving me today. I hope that you enjoy it here at the palace...and thank you for what you will do in the future," she said, smiling at me so brightly that I wondered how her cheeks didn't break off.

She gave me a small little smile, a soft blush to her cheeks as she looked at me.

She finally let me go, and a maid directed me to my chambers the next door down the hall from her own.

What...what did all of this mean?

I opened my chamber door, and I was in awe by how clean and neat the room was.

There was a luxurious bed, posts draped with beautiful sheer, purple curtains. The bed was filled with rich, high-quality, stunning white blankets with purple accents; the colors of the imperial mage family, the Sultan, and his Sultana.

The walls were bright, painted white with gold and purple accents.

Candles lined the white-wooden dresser, and a beautiful, large chandelier with at least one hundred mage-light orbs lit the room from the center.

Mage light orbs were not a new invention—the mage light spell had been evolved, into an orb that you could use like a candle, and the pure white glow gave the room an even brighter look.

I thought I would try my hand at turning off the chandelier...because we didn't have one of these at Qassim's home.

"...*Zalaam*," I said, and the chandelier immediately responded, darkening right away, leaving only the burning candles.

I smiled. I could get used to this.

I sighed, and stepped over to the bed. I noticed a shimmery, sleek robe made of satin, and I smiled again as I pulled off my tunic and pants, and the maid left the room with it, taking it to be laundered.

I pulled on the robe, and plopped down into the bed, before a small knock came at the door.

I called in the maid, who brought me a tray of delicious looking foods, and made sure I didn't need anything else before directing me to leave my dishes on the small round dining table in the corner of the room when I was finished.

I ate in peace, and enjoyed the solitude for a bit, stepping out onto the balcony of my chambers.

The balcony overlooked the courtyard, with its wonderful gardens and fountains, an aviary...

This was the life.

I hadn't ever been here, to the palace, but when I had heard Qassim talk of its splendor, I had always wondered.

It was a special honor for someone who wasn't a royal to be able to see it.

It did strike me as odd, though...I felt more at home, *here*, than I had ever felt at Qassim's.

The environment makes the man, I guess?

I looked up to the stars, before I stepped back inside and curled up into bed, enjoying the amazingly soft matte satin damask designs on jacquard-woven polyester chenille. It was a corded comforter with a color-matched cotton and polyester backing. The bedding filler seemed to be polyester.

Top of the line quality, high-dollar, high-class material that had likely been imported.

I wasn't even a member of the royal family.

I was, simply, a child found and raised by the palace sorcerer who had fled his position after his masters had been slain and found solace in peaceful, charitable work in the kingdom.

I was nothing…nobody.

To think that my good deed had managed to bring me to this place, with these amazing amenities and amazing food…

I was in total bliss.

I had never experienced this kind of life before, but somehow…I felt like I was truly home for the first time.

The next morning arrived too soon, and I sat up, rubbing my eyes.

It was still dark, but I could tell from the pink that was streaking along the horizon that the sun would be up soon enough.

Dawn wasn't far behind that light.

I glanced to see that the tray that I had eaten my meal from the night before had vanished, and I smiled. That maid was quiet...

A bit *too* quiet.

I was usually a very light sleeper.

"*Anar*," I spoke the word for "illuminate," and the chandelier blazed to life.

I stood, making the bed, and stepping over to the dresser to find a mannikin at the side, dressed in a set of training gear.

I took if off the dummy, dressing myself in a tunic, topping it off with the training gear.

I glanced at myself in the mirror nearby, and startled.

I looked like a different person, dressed in something like this. I was not used to this.

I usually only wore tunics and robes, of mid-class qualities.

This wasn't even clothing that the royal family wore, but it was still of higher quality than anything I'd ever owned.

A small knock sounded on the door, and I opened it to find the maid there, with a tray of breakfast.

"I heard you'd awaken early, and need food before you left for training at sunrise. I also need to guide you to the training hall."

I smiled, nodding. "Thank you, um...?"

"I am Amal Hashim. I am a lower nobleman's daughter, gifted to her highness as a handmaiden. We have been friends since we were old enough to walk," she laughed.

"Ah, I see," I said, nodding.

She blushed as she looked at me, and I took in her features. She had a soft round face, with light brown hair, and golden-brown eyes.

She was quite pretty, but I wasn't here to form bonds like these...and if she was, that would be a problem.

"The princess wanted her personal team to be close together. I will be assisting you—unless, of course, you would rather have a servant boy. One of those can be arranged, too!" She said quickly. "But I thought it would be nice for me to assist you, since I am good friends with the princess. She needs a close-knit team, right?"

I considered this. "I will think over that."

I ate the food she had brought me—a traditional breakfast of grilled sliced eggplant, rolled to hold ricotta cheese and chopped mint leaves, four hard boiled eggs, and a handful of olives and cherry tomatoes.

I kicked back a glass of Amar al Din—an apricot juice prepared with orange blossom water.

Then, she had another maid come to take the tray away and she led me through the halls and out to the court outside, through there, and into a long building.

Chapter 3 — Klaus

I glanced around, and noticed that I was here before anyone else.

"Lord Amir should be here shortly." She turned, giving a bow before she walked away.

I began to stretch, pulling my muscles tight and feeling some pops here and there.

I heard the steps approach me quickly, and I turned just in time to see a fist flying toward my face.

I stepped back and caught the fist, and I saw Amir's wide eyes and slightly gaping mouth.

"She was right. You are more skilled than I would have accredited you." He gave a nod, standing back upright. "Good. Very good." He looked me up and down, an…unplaceable expression on his face. "…How old are you?"

"I'm four—"

"I thought so," he said, cutting me off and crossing his arms. "Who is your father?"

For some reason, alarm bells began to ring in my head, and I wanted to keep the information to myself…because something, deep in my gut, told me that this man knew way more than he let on.

He looked at me as if he knew exactly who I was, without me saying a word.

I felt this strange weight in the put of my stomach when he looked at me with those eyes.

"...I think you already know," I said.

He quirked a brow for a moment before he smirked at me. "You are correct; I do. You are the son of Qassim Malik."

I gaped at him for a second. "You...really did know?"

He chuckled. "I did. There is only one family with that surname in the royal city."

"Oh," I said, though I didn't buy it that this was the only reason that he knew who my father was.

"Qassim was once regarded as the highest-level sorcerer in the palace. He was a master, and he was fervently dedicated to the Sultan and his Sultana until their deaths. Then, he gave his notice of leave and has faded into the wayside, irrelevant." He lost the smirk on his face. "Which will you be, I wonder? A power to be reckoned with, dedicated to the royal family? A nobody on the sidelines, with no one who will know who you are? Or...something else, entirely?"

I eyed him. "...I don't suppose you're going to tell me what that third option is?"

He chuckled. "Maybe...if you can prove to me that you can earn it." He shrugged. "As it stands, I have no reason to tell you anything I know."

I felt my energy blaze, and I glared at him.

"Hm," he said, eyes narrowing as he smirked and gave a nod, appraising me. "Yes, good. Keep that spirit about you. You'll need it." Then, he glanced around the training hall. "Are you proficient with magics, yet? What spells can you perform? As a Malik, I assume you must be well-versed."

I hesitated. "...I can't use it."

"Pardon?" He asked, surprised.

"There is a problem with my mana. I don't have my mana roots, and so my power is not solidifying properly," I said, opting to be honest, since he was my trainer. "I have been training hard, and working on physical activity and light combat, and I know many spells...but I can't apply those yet."

He, shockingly, did not look surprised at this information. He had looked surprised about not being able to use my mana, but the reason did not surprise him...

Why did he not look surprised?

"That makes sense, if you're adopted."

I felt surprise run through me. "How did you—?"

"You look nothing like Qassim, nor his wife or other children. It is not a hard guess," he said, rolling his eyes. He finally sighed, glancing out the window, before he looked back to me and entered a defensive pose. "Come, then. Show me everything you know. Show me, boy...what *you can do*."

The rest of the day passed without so much as a break for a meal, and it ended with me finishing my one hundredth lap around the training hall after night had fallen, and all the other palace warriors had already retired to their chambers for the night.

Amir sat back, leaning back in a lounge chair, eyeing me with crossed arms as I finished my laps.

He leisurely sipped on his glass of wine, raising an eyebrow as I trotted over to him.

"Go back to your chambers, now…and meet me at sunrise."

I nearly groaned, but the blow he'd made to the side of my head earlier when I had groaned over an instruction made me reconsider.

I gave a respectful bow. "Thank you for your guidance, Lord Amir," I said. "I will see you first thing in the morning."

He watched me with narrowed eyes, and didn't respond other than giving a tight nod.

I turned, and startled at the handmaiden who happened to be standing there, with a tray in her hands that held a warm wet towel.

Her name was Amal, if I remembered correctly. She was the princess's friend and handmaiden, who had been selected by the princess to become my handmaiden and assist me.

I wasn't sure how well that would work out, considering how excited she was to be in my presence…

"How was training?" She asked, a smile on her face.

"…Eventful," I said without much feeling at her overly excited manner and the blush on her cheeks.

She was too excited to see me.

I needed to let her known that I wasn't someone she needed to be close to. I could see it in her posture and expressions, she meant to pursue me.

I knew that I was good looking, but I definitely wasn't interested in that.

She stepped to the side, and was much too close to my body. She was close to *touching* me, she was hovering so near around me.

I didn't like it.

I sighed, and turned to fully face her.

"You need to take a step back," I said, soft, and I watched her eyes go wide as her brows lifted, a look of surprise on her face.

"W…what?"

"…You need to step away from me," I told her, meeting her gaze. "You are too close to me."

Hurt flashed in her eyes, and she looked down at the ground before she shuffled back half a step.

"Further."

Shock flashed on her face. "Huh?"

"Step back further," I said, more force in my tone.

She gaped back at me. "Why?"

"Because," I said, stepping away myself and shooting her a cold look "You are too close."

Some form of dignity seemed to ignite. "Oh," she said, clasping her hands behind her back. "You don't like close physical presence, then?" She asked, hopefulness in her face and a blush on her cheeks.

"...I don't like you being so close to me."

There. I'd said it.

Her eyebrows pulled down sharply, and her eyes got sad...but more than that, her blush deepened.

I'd embarrassed her.

"I am sorry if I was too close, too fast. I just wanted to be close to you. I actually asked the princess to make *me* your personal handmaiden instead of the one she planned to assign, you know...not out of having any sinister or bad intentions, but because I'm really interested in—"

"*I* am not interested in *you* in such a way. I am sorry, but that isn't something that I seek."

She scoffed. "Oh, why not? Am I not pretty enough? I am close to the princess!" She said, giving me a scathing look. "You're a commoner. You'd be foolish to turn down someone like me."

I cocked a brow at her. "…I was raised by one of the most renowned sorcerers in the country, whom once had the top sorcerer position in this very palace. I don't need to be with you to be somebody in this place. And, it isn't that you aren't pretty. I am sure a man out there will be very happy to be with you one day…but I am not that man, and I need you to know something very important; I am here to do a job. I am not here to make friends and enter relationships. I am here to be a guard for the princess—that is all."

"…I don't think you know what you're doing," she seethed.

"And I don't think you're the maiden who needs to be attending to me," I said, making a mental note as I walked away to request that the princess switch my handmaiden.

"You're so rude!" She said in a harsh breath, turning and rushing off the other direction.

I made my way through the halls, and managed to find myself at the princess's door. I knocked lightly, and her other handmaiden answered the door.

"Oh, it is you!" She said, giving a bow of her head. "I hope your training went well today. The princess is inside, please," she said, stepping over to allow me inside. "Princess, your new guard has arrived."

"Oh, good, good!" The princess said, smiling brightly and stepping over. "You look good in uniform!" She grinned. "Training?"

"It went well," I told her, bowing. "He was tough, but fair. I am sure I will become stronger under his guidance quickly." I glanced at her. "I do, however, have something else that I need to address, your highness."

"Oh?" She asked, eyes bright and warm.

I swallowed. "I would like to humbly request that my attendant be changed."

"Oh?" She asked, brows shooting up in surprise. "Did Amal offend you?"

"Well…" I sighed. "She made an advance upon me, and got in my space. She became very rude when I informed her that I did not, in fact, hold mutual interest in her in a romantic aspect."

"Ahaha! Hahaha!" She laughed "Yes, I wondered how you may respond to that. She requested that she be made your attendant, rather than my other handmaiden, and was adamant that she was very smitten with you. I honestly thought she needed to be brought down a peg when she said that you'd be a fool to not desire her." She shrugged. "I am sorry that I let her attend to you. I didn't actually think she'd be brave enough to act this quickly, but it appears she was more brazen than I had originally thought."

"It is alright, your highness. I simply told her the truth—I am your guard. I am not interested in pursuing romance in the palace…and I was not interested in her, in particular. She insisted that I was ignorant and that, as a commoner, I should not turn her down."

"Oh, my," she giggled. "Being turned down by a 'commoner' must have hurt her pride a bit." She nodded. "Yes, I will change your attendant. Would you prefer a male?"

"If that is alright," I told her. "I know that, as princess, most of your attendants and employees that you oversee are female."

"It isn't a problem at all," she smiled at me. "I have two servant boys whom I have attending to the garden and aviary now, just keeping it cleaned up. You may choose one of them, or both, if you wish. With that brazen attitude, perhaps I can assign Amal to the garden and aviary care for a while. She shouldn't have been so rude. She was lucky that I gave her permission to attend to you in the first place." She sighed, glancing at her other handmaiden. "Please go to the servant chambers and request for those two." The handmaiden scurried off, and the princess turned back to me. "Those boys should be good to work for you. They will probably enjoy that work over cleaning the garden and watching after the birds," she grinned.

"Thank you, princess," I said, bowing at the waist. "I appreciate this."

A few minutes later, the other handmaiden arrived with two boys following her. They couldn't have been much older than ten years old, either of them.

"Go ahead and introduce yourselves," she told them.

One was darker skinned than the other, with thick, curly brown hair and bright, vivid hazel eyes. He gave a bow. "I am Hamir," he said.

The other was a milder, lighter toned brown, and he had sleek, cheek-long black hair. His eyes were more of a golden, honey-glazed color. He bowed. "My name is Azmin," he told me.

I smiled at them. "It is nice to meet you both. I am Klaus Malik, and I have requested to have male attendants. How would you both like to work for me?"

Their eyes. Lit. Up.

"Really?" They asked simultaneously.

I chuckled. "Yes. It isn't very exciting work, but it should be a little more to do than cleaning the garden and the aviary—"

"You mean we get to clean armor, polish weapons, and help a guard?" Azmin asked.

"And we get to talk to a warrior and have time around a man?" Hamir asked.

I glanced at the princess, who gave me a sheepish expression. "I admit, the work I was having them do wasn't very stimulating. It was rather boring."

I grinned as my attention returned to the boys in front of me. "Are you both sure you wish to work for me? You know that as a guard to the princess, my life will be in danger and that my attendants will also be obligated to help me protect the princess?" I asked.

They both nodded quickly, enthusiastic.

Excited.

I gave a nod, and smiled at them. "Alright, then. Welcome to my service," I said, holding out my hand, and they each took a turn shaking it. "Get some good rest for tonight, and be sure to come to my chambers with breakfast well before dawn, so that I have time to eat and leave for training before sunrise."

"Yes, sir!" They said, bowing before they scurried off.

I chuckled, and turned back to the princess. "Thank you again, your highness."

She smiled. "Will you be alright for the evening?"

I nodded. "I am not hungry at the moment. I will go draw myself a bath, and then settle in for the night. I will have an early day, tomorrow."

"Alright," she told me. "Goodnight, Klaus."

"Goodnight, your highness."

Chapter 4 — Claudianne Jakard

"He is your responsibility. You will see to his living arrangements, his food, his training...everything. You will be the Sultana, once you marry, and this will be a good chance to give you some authority and responsibility to see how well you handle being in charge of people." He threw one more glance at the boy, before he turned, and began to walk away.

I rushed over to the boy, smiling brightly with as much welcoming warmth I could muster after almost being kidnapped. "Come, come! I will take you back to the palace with me and show you where you'll be staying."

"W-wait, I—"

"Come, you'll love the palace! I'll be sure that you are well taken care of!" I said, not listening in the slightest. I was terrified that he would refuse to come with me, and with everything going on in my life and only having one true guard, I didn't feel safe.

I had been very specifically targeted, and if he hadn't been there...

I shuttered to think about it.

With no further protest, he followed me slowly, albeit with a guarded stance and uncomfortable expression on his face.

I would just have to try to make sure he was as comfortable as possible...because I hadn't felt this safe in a long time.

I knew, despite my age, how much danger I was in a the only remaining blood-relation to the former sultan and sultana...and how much misfortune had befallen my family line since before my birth.

I was a huge target. I'd have to be a fool not to realize.

"You want to be his attendant?" I asked, giving her a look.

"Please? Please, please, please, your highness?" She begged me, on her knees. "He's so handsome, and he's only a commoner! He would be lucky to even beg for my hand, and yet, here I am, offering my hand on my own!" She giggled. "He would be foolish to turn me down."

I glanced at my other handmaiden, who shrugged and went back to preparing tea.

I sighed, and sincerely hoped that my new guard would put this girl in her place.

"Fine," I said, rubbing my hands with lotion. "I suppose that it can't hurt anything." I shrugged. "If that's what you want to do."

She gleefully left the room, and my other handmaiden and I laughed, shaking our heads.

"She is much too haughty for our age group," I said, sighing.

"I kind of hope he knocks her down a peg!" My best friend snickered.

I nodded. "Yes, that would be good for her; to be humbled by a 'mere commoner.' Please," I said, rolling my eyes.

"Thank you again, your highness," he said, and flashed a bright smile that had my heart giving a strange pulse in my chest.

He turned, and left the room with his two new attendant boys.

I grinned at my best friend and closest handmaiden, Saffora Setz. Her sleek black hair was pulled back into a braid, and her bright hazel eyes sparkled as she met my smile.

"That didn't take long," she giggled.

"I knew that Amal wouldn't last long attending to him," I sighed, shrugging. "She's definitely not of a good disposition for that kind of thing—not getting her way, I mean," I laughed softly.

"Too bad for her, because, mm, mm, mm...that man is so delicious."

I burst out into giggles. "Saffora!" I grinned at her. "Oh, was your elder sister's marriage decided on?" I asked.

We had been in the midst of discussing the plans for my marriage, when she mentioned that her parents were marrying off her elder sister. They were a noble family as well, and they had two daughters—Saffora and Fatima.

She sighed. "They have a few people in mind, but nothing definite, yet."

I sighed, too. I was not very happy with my prospects, so far.

Aran Hassan, a very powerful swordsman who was the son of a powerful lord in a neighboring kingdom...and very arrogant and rude.

Then, the most appealing to my father, and the one whom they *intended* to wed me to, as far as I had heard—Kasha Fazar.

He was the son of a duke, and though I had only met him once, he had made my skin crawl.

He was too...too...suave.

He was too perfect.

Well-mannered. Calm. Bright but cold feeling golden eyes that reminded me of the metal...or a snake.

That's exactly the vibe that I got from him; a cold, deceitful, slithering snake seeking the next poor, defenseless rat it wanted to consume...and I was the rat.

Except, I wasn't a rat, and I shouldn't feel like I was prey.

He was scheduled to come in a week, to spend the day with me and make a final decision on whether or not he would propose marriage to our family.

I was not looking forward to his visit.

The one time I had seen him, he had been perfectly respectable, but too cold. His conversation had sounded so rehearsed and fake...

I shuttered thinking about it.

Saffora and I continued talking about things...our concerns, our joys, and telling one another things only we could discuss without judgment. Things I couldn't trust to tell Amal.

Then, we fell asleep together, tired and spent from crying.

"So, how is his training coming along?" I heard my father's voice in his office from my place in the hall.

It had been a couple of days, and my possible fiancé was due to arrive in only three more days.

I was so anxious, and I had to try to make an appeal to my father...because I didn't want to marry this man.

Amir's voice followed. "It is coming along far better than I had anticipated. He is quick on the uptake, and much stronger than I would have thought, considering his age and lack of training."

"You are sure he said that his last name was Malik?"

"Yes," Amir said. "But he has already confirmed that he is adopted. I guessed it, and he told me it was true. Despite both having sorcerer's hair, they still look nothing alike."

"Hm. Have you contacted Qassim, yet? Was he shocked to learn where he is?"

"Yes, I have contacted him. He was, as I predicted, unsurprised to learn that he had made it to the palace…he didn't give me any response as to why this didn't surprise him."

"Hm…"

"Your grace," Amir trailed off. "Do you…do you think the boy is—"

"That is what I am leaning toward, but without proof or without a confession, I can't completely say. Confirmation that he's adopted is fine and well, but that doesn't tell me with one hundred percent certainty that he is…*that*." My father sighed heavily. "We weren't there that night."

"If he is, though, that would make him—"

"Hush!" Father scolded. "Be careful of speaking such information. You know the history, better than many of the other servants and guards in this palace. Speaking such things…could spell more danger."

"So," Amir said, his voice contemplative. "Are you really going to allow him to be her guard? If he really is who we suspect he might be, then that would make him—"

"Yes," my father said. "If nothing else, to keep them *both* close and safe. Nothing good could come from revealing his possible identity right now. We need to keep it a secret, and also…I want to speak to Qassim myself—"

"He refused to come in, unless directly summoned by the royal, herself…"

Father scoffed. "Of course, he did. Qassim was always like that—loyal to only the *direct bloodline*. He won't speak to me unless my daughter orders it, hm?" Father sighed. "Of course. Things cannot just be easy."

"To think that he would be under our noses, all this time…if he *is* who we suspect, anyway," Amir said, sounding exasperated. "But with that hair, those *eyes*—"

"Yes," father said. "But it doesn't make sense, either."

"Your grace?"

"All the bodies were accounted for. If they'd had another, we should have known—"

"They did have several, so it might be possible that we missed—"

I moved to step away, and I startled with a cry of fright when the door ripped open completely and Amir rushed into the hall, sword drawn.

"W-wait!" I cried, hands up in surrender.

"Your highness…?" Amir said, surprised. "What—"

"I came to talk to my father…"

He sighed, and my father called out for me to come on inside from his office.

"So, how long have you been sneaking around out there like a rat?" My father asked, and I flinched at his eyebrow rising…giving me a look of resignation and irritation.

"…I wasn't intending to eavesdrop, father. I am sorry. I had come to speak with you—"

"Regarding what?"

"…My impending marriage…"

He let out a groan. "I've told you already, Claudianne, we are not having this discussion any further. You are getting married. You need to ascend to the throne as the sultana, and soon. The palace, if you haven't noticed, is out of sorts and the kingdom needs order. I've done the best that I can as a stand-in, but I am no sultan…and, your mother is not long for this word."

"Do I *have* to marry in order to get to the throne, fa—?"

"Yes," he said, tone firm. "That is the law. An unmarried woman cannot become sultana."

I sighed, and he slammed his hand on his desk. I startled, and I felt my shoulders slouch.

"Your mother cannot help me rule this nation, no matter how much I wish it were so, Claudianne. She's on her deathbed," he said, his eyes filling with tears. "I always wanted to stay with only one woman. I never anticipated that we'd end up in this position, and I never thought that she'd end up so sick. Without her, I do not hold any authority…"

"Father, I don't like—"

"You will grow to like whomever it is that you end up marrying. I do not expect you to like him right away. All you need to worry about is having someone powerful to help you rule."

"But, father—"

"That's the end of it. You will be respectful when the ducal heir arrives in three days."

"Papa..." I whispered, eyes burning my eyes. "He gives me a bad feeling—"

"Enough!" He shouted. "This isn't up for discussion anymore. This is it."

"But—"

"Go to your chambers," he said, scolding tone. He looked to Amir. "Escort her...and do not let her leave her chambers for the rest of the night."

"Yes, your grace," Amir said, bowing at the waist before he turned and held out his arm for me.

I looped my arm with his, and he led me through the halls of the palace to my chambers without saying anything.

When we arrived to my chambers, I stiffly opened the doors and shuffled inside.

"For what it is worth, princess," he said, and I glanced at his handsome face. "I agree with you. You shouldn't have to marry to earn the position."

My eyes watered, and I gave him a hug. "Thank you, Amir."

"You're welcome. Goodnight, your highness," he said, pressing a kiss into my hair and giving a bow at the waist. Then, he turned, and crossed the hall to his own chambers.

The palace was abuzz, what with the arrival of the son of Duke Fazar—Kasha.

Food was being prepared, guards prepped and readied to be on alert, and my maidens dressing me to the nicest of their ability.

I looked as if I were being made into a bride, but realistically…I knew that I, in fact, was.

Kasha had not made an official proposal yet, but my father had already made it clear his intentions on the matter—if Kasha did so happen to propose, my father would accept it on my behalf.

Period.

No other discussion necessary.

That's why he insisted that I look my very best, and to be on my absolute best behavior…so as not to offend him in any way.

That had been the original hangup all along; me.

Kasha had been sent by his father six months ago, when word of "my" seeking a husband had first come to light.

His father, Duke Karim Fazar, had wanted a closer relationship to my father, Archduke Jakard. He wanted trading deals and to be closer to the palace in his connections.

Kasha had been sent to make his interest in marrying me known...that is, until I had pitched a huge tantrum about it.

I had made it clear to him and his father that I wasn't seeking marriage, nor was I comfortable around Kasha.

Kasha was six years older than I was, so it wasn't a huge age difference, that was true...but his mentality and his behavior was totally different than my own.

I felt my skin crawl around him.

I would turn thirteen in the coming March, but he had just turned twenty.

He was an adult. He was popular with women, too.

He would, likely, demand to have concubines...most men would. I was no fool...and...

When he looked at me, I felt like my skin was burning...and not in a pleasant way.

I felt naked around him.

I glanced at myself in the mirror, and I shuttered a bit.

"Is something wrong, your highness?" The eldest handmaiden asked—a woman who normally helped my mother to get ready, and was here to gift me with something from my mother for good luck.

There was a lot wrong, but I didn't bother to voice this.

I wore a flimsy outfit that was, in my opinion, more suited to the dancers of the court than a princess.

The light purple bedlah halter top with an attached hood and veil, where my sides, shoulders and arms, and my back where all exposed.

My torso, however, was covered with a sheer, see-through material covered in sequins that led down to a bodice skirt that had slits down the draped sides, leaving the sides of my legs exposed as well. Over the expanse of the skirt that left almost nothing to the imagination, was a sheer skirt that flowed over the entire bottom.

Arm bands around my biceps held delicate strings with sequins that connected to wrist bands.

My feet were covered by white leather strap sandals that rose up my calves and were covered in delicate amethyst stone sequins.

My silvery hair was pulled into a rose-shaped bun right behind my ear, with the rest of my hair spilling out beneath it like a waterfall of silver waves over my shoulder.

My eyes were lined with eyeliner and mascara, and my eyelids painted a deep, dark smoky grey. My lips were stained with deep purple rouge.

I looked...like a harem bride, almost.

Anger spiked in me.

I didn't like this. I didn't want to look like this. I didn't want to be engaged to this man, and I certainly didn't want to marry him. I didn't even want to feel his eyes on me; that gaze that made my skin crawl like I was covered in centipedes.

They spritzed a dash of rose-oil on me, for scent…and then, I was led out of the room.

We stopped and knocked on Klaus' door, and he opened the door up and followed us, armed and in uniform.

It took everything in me to keep my eyes trained on the maid in front of me, leading us through the halls, while I felt his warm gaze upon me.

I knew what I must look like, even as the sequins on my dress were shimmering in the lights of the corridors.

Yes, I was sure this was the kind of girls that Kasha must like; harem girls.

No princess should look like a harem girl, though, and it angered me.

I may not have been a princess for long, but I had always been groomed for a position like it, and I knew that this…this was not normal.

Would my father even be able to see me in this without throwing a fit? Vomiting, even?

My breasts were pushed together and mushed to make cleavage, for heaven's sake!

When we arrived to the throne room, I stepped up to the throne and gave a gentle curtsy to my father.

"Father, I have arrived to your summons," I said, keeping my voice as even as I could manage.

"Raise your head, daughter," he said, his voice oddly thick.

I did so, and noticed Kasha at his side, his eyes half-mast and a thick swallow at his throat.

He was clenching his left hand, discreetly, just behind his left thigh.

He wanted to touch me…

I felt naked beneath his heady gaze, and I tried to keep my dignity and forced myself not to fidget. I was nervous, and uncomfortable.

"Aren't you going to welcome Lord Kasha?" My father asked, impatient, and I flinched a little, giving another nod toward him.

"Hello, Lord Kasha," I said, soft.

He paused, waiting for me to continue, but when I didn't, he scoffed. "That's it, princess? No, 'it is an honor to see you again,' or 'it is nice to see you again?'" He sighed. "Well, no matter. Let us adjourn to have supper. I am starving," he smirked.

He stepped up to me, and offered out his hand…which, with a glare from my father when I glanced nervously at his outstretched hand, I finally took and let him lead me through the halls, following the maids.

My father…did not follow us.

He actually left me alone with this man!

We reached the dining room, and sat down to be served.

"So, then. How is life adjusting in the palace? Have you considered what choice you will make, if I do indeed extend a proposal?"

I tried not to glare at him. "I don't have the luxury of making a decision," I told him.

"Perhaps not, but you are the bride."

"...What about it?"

"'What about it?' Surely, you know that marrying *me* is the best option. What was your other option, again? Starving and rotting with the rest of the kingdom and refusing to marry, letting another come in and claim it for themselves and remove the title from your bloodline? Or, what, marrying a weaker lord who isn't of the proper disposition to rule? Letting me marry you and give you the power and authority you need to become the sultana is the most profitable and sensible outcome, isn't it?"

I hated that silver, forked-tongue of his, spieling on and making such a convincing argument.

I knew that he was right, realistically, but I hated that heated golden gaze that swept over me...the fluid, graceful manner in which he spoke...the shoulders that were broad and pulled back, head raised high and chin upward as if he were better than me, looking down at me.

He made my skin crawl.

He was too perfect; there had to be something wrong with him. Some horrible, critical flaw.

He made me instantly think of a villain, hiding behind a target in plain sight and whispering sweet words in their ear, even as he brings up a knife to slit their throat.

There was just something about him that made me uncomfortable.

I didn't respond, and he let out a silky sounding chuckle, but didn't press it.

We ate the meal in silence, before I gave a curtsy as I stood. "I am ready to retire for the evening," I informed. "The attendants will show you to your guest chambers."

"Do you not wish to hear my final decision?" He asked, fingers lacing and chin resting on the back of his hands, elbows resting on the table.

I trembled minutely. "I am sure my father will let me know, as soon as you tell him. Good evening," I said, turning to leave with my guard and handmaiden at my side.

"I am sending the proposal," he said, and I froze. "You'd be wise…not to fight this any further. This is the best option for all involved. If you will set aside your pride, and realize your position," he said, standing and approaching me, and he lay a hand on my shoulder, standing behind me and leaning in to speak quietly in my ear. When my guard went to unsheathe his sword, I held up my hand, making him pause. "I will take care of you…see to your needs…and be the powerful sultan to stand as a pillar for my sultana," he breathed.

I trembled, and alarm bells rang in my head…my skin prickled, and all the hair on my body stood on end.

My eyes burned, and I tugged away from him. "Good evening, Lord Fazar." Then, I walked with great speed out of the room, my chest tight as sobs threatened to spill out.

"Your highness," Saffora murmured, holding my hand and squeezing as we rushed through the halls.

"I…I don't…" I choked out, and I shuttered. I took a deep breath, and let it out slowly. "I don't have any choices, Saffora. Father has told me already, if Lord Kasha proposes…he will accept it…! I don't want…I don't…!" I sobbed.

We reached my chambers, finally, and I rushed into the room and collapsed to the floor, even as Klaus rushed to shut the door and come over to me, at my side.

"Your highness," Saffora whispered, taking me into a hug and stroking my back. "It will be alright," she said.

Sobs bubbled up and out of me, and I broke down crying in her arms.

Chapter 5 – Claudianne

"I understand," I murmured the following day, looking at my family's painting on the wall behind my father's desk in his office.

My eyes were swollen from crying all night, and I didn't even bother putting on makeup today. I wore a thick cloak, refusing to dress up today after yesterday. If I had to get married, I at least wanted to be comfortable wearing what I wanted. Perhaps this would protect me from Kasha's eyes.

My father studied me, letting out a soft breath and looking away. "He's been groomed for leadership, Claudianne. He will be a good partner for you."

I didn't respond. I just gave a tight nod, and felt my spirit listless and unfeeling inside me.

"Claudianne," father said. "Don't cry," he told me.

Was I crying…? I hadn't thought that I was.

"Your marriage will take place when you turn thirteen."

"W…what…so soon?" I asked, horrified. "But that—"

"That's six months. You have six months, Claudianne, to get used to the idea and come to terms with it. During that time, Lord Kasha will be visiting periodically to spend a few days, and spend time with you. You will open up to him, in time, I am sure. Have I ever told you that your mother was an arranged marriage for me?"

I glanced up at him. I had been told, in the past, but I didn't have any real details about their interaction.

To be honest, most marriages among nobles were arranged, so that was just a reality that I had to face, being the one person left in the royal bloodline to rise to the throne.

"Your mother wasn't very excited about marrying me, either. She fought the sultan, insisting that she not have to marry. Being the only daughter of the sultan, with two elder brothers...she felt that she shouldn't have to leave home and be married. But, if she hadn't...there would be nobody left of the original imperial bloodline to ascend the throne. It was difficult, and we didn't get along for quite a while. She fought me a lot, and then one day...I was injured by a radical against the mages, while I was protecting your mother. With her silver hair, despite not having studied sorcery arts, she had been targeted. After that, she began to open up to me. We became quite close, and you came along not long after."

I hadn't known that...

"I didn't know that you weren't close..." I said. "She didn't want to marry you?"

He smiled softly, shaking his head. "No...but I proved myself, and she warmed up to me. The fruit of those labors and struggles was born, and has grown into a beautiful young woman who is now coming into her own blossoming time." He came over to me, pulling me into a hug. "Please, darling...try. Try not to fight him too much. He may just be the right one for you."

I had to try to push myself to see it from his viewpoint.

My father and mother had been in an arranged marriage, and it hadn't been rainbows and sunshine when they were first put together, as it turns out.

As a man who had been arranged to a princess—who had been vehemently against marrying him—if she hadn't warmed up to him, I likely wouldn't exist. Since I had been born, they had always been close. He had never treated her wrongly.

He had never had mistresses, as far as I was aware.

He had always treated my mother as if she were his moonlight to his sunshine. Necessary and beautiful and powerful.

My mother had been a very happy, smiling, peaceful woman all my life...seeing her so ill ripped our hearts apart.

I was about to become the true last member of the imperial bloodline...oh, how our family had fallen.

I, unfortunately, had never gotten to meet any of my family, either. My mother, despite having lost her parents, siblings, and the rest, had always been cheerful and warm and trusting.

This entire situation was a mess.

My father, for the first time, was pushing me into something I didn't want...he'd always been wrapped around my little finger, and I'd always been a big daddy's girl, but then mother got sick...and her older brothers had both already died.

She could not ascend the throne, and so it fell to me. Father turned cold and hard, firm, and began working with me to prepare me for the role and knowing my place as the princess.

Everything had changed. Eating, sleeping, holding myself, all that had remained similar...as the daughter of the Archduke and Archduchess, I would marry a high-ranked man one day, anyway...but to become sultana?

It was on a much higher scale.

I could understand why my father was so serious, no matter how much it hurt me. The entire situation hurt me.

I was only twelve.

My mother had been bedridden for quite a long time, and was not doing well. Father was in a rush to see me wed and in position so that he could spend what time she had left with her, at her side.

I sighed, and gave a soft nod. "I…will try to…not fight with him or hate him…" I said.

"Good," he said, and he pressed a kiss to my forehead. "I know that a lot is happening. It hasn't been long since we moved to the palace, and everything changed. Life became about helping you ascend to the throne, and ruling a nation…I know how much pressure that is, on top of your mother's sickness. But everything…" He took in a deep inhale, and let it out, slowly. He did it a couple more times, walking me through calming breaths. "Everything will turn out alright. I promise."

Several days passed, and I now stood outside in the courtyard as Lord Kasha mounted his horse, prepping to leave the palace for his family home for now.

As his fiancé, I was now obligated to welcome him and send him off.

He smirked at me from his place on his beautiful, rich, tan brown Caspian horse with black, thick mane and tail, a splash of black on the face, and black legs.

It reminded me of him, actually.

"I have an idea of an engagement gift for you," he smirked at me, appraising me as I admired his horse. "I will see you in a month," he told me, before he and his guards turned and left.

A gift...

What gift could give me?

"Your highness?" Klaus spoke up, and I turned to him. "How are you feeling?"

I looked around, and noticed that all of the other servants had gone. It was Klaus and I, alone, in the courtyard.

I smiled at him. "I am alright, thank you, Klaus. I feel a little drained for some reason, but otherwise, not bad."

He smiled and gave me a bow.

"I have something for you," I told him, and I reached into my pocket and pulled out a leather wristband that had a dark, thick amethyst stone embedded in it.

"Oh, your highness," he said, and I felt a warm tingle in my hand where his skin brushed against mine, and I felt this warm heaviness fill my chest.

This couldn't be a coincidence. I'd felt something similar when he'd hugged me, too, and his reaction had also been a bit strange.

He reacted much the same, now...a feeling of peace crossing his handsome features, though he schooled it to hide it.

What did this mean...?

"Thank you," he told me, smiling at me. "Amethyst is my—"

"I know," I smiled at him. "I, uh, remembered you saying that, before. I wanted to get this for you, to help you with your mana training."

"Thank you," he said, bowing. "Thank you, your highness."

"Thank you for your hard work," I beamed at him.

We made our way back through the halls, without speaking again for a long while. We finally reached my chambers, and stood just outside.

It was still just us, even in the hall.

I turned to face him, and met his eyes.

He held my gaze, and it took a long...long, long moment before we both seemingly startled out of it at the sound of a door far down the hall closing shut loudly.

I realized, glancing down, that my hand and his had subconsciously reached out toward one another, close to touching.

I could feel the heat rising from his skin.

"Oh," I murmured, glancing up to meet his eyes again.

I hadn't ever met another person outside of my own family who had purple eyes...it wasn't common.

It was almost impossible, really.

The only people in our nation said to hold that eye-color were, in fact, members of the imperial family...but he wasn't part of the imperial family. His father was a marquis leveled civilian sorcerer.

He wasn't a nobleman...certainly not a royal.

It made no sense.

"Well, good evening, princess. If you need anything, please alert me right away."

I grinned at him. "Yes, I will. Thank you."

"And," he said as an afterthought. "If you ever need someone to talk to about anything...I am happy to listen."

"Thank you, Klaus."

I stepped into my room, and as I wandered over to my bed, I let myself revel in the tingles that had rose all the way through my body at the feeling of his skin touching mine.

It wasn't a normal reaction, was it? I hadn't ever felt this way with anyone else...and certainly, it wasn't the same as the unpleasant, skin-crawling feeling I got when my fiancé just looked at me.

No, this feeling was warm and cozy and...and *home*.

I would think that I were under a spell of some kind, had I not known for a fact that he couldn't practice sorcery right now.

Which was another thing—though I wasn't well versed in the magic arts, I had no issues practicing my magic because of my root sources.

What was the problem with his root sources?

Shouldn't he have full access to his mana network? He had a loving family at home, right?

So many unanswered questions that clouded my thoughts.

Thoughts of this handsome, striking young man who made me feel warm and cozy and at peace...

It was perplexing.

October, 139 IY

"I am pleased to see you in such good health, dear Claud," Lord Kasha smirked at me, and I sighed, giving a small curtsy.

"Yes," I said, simply.

I could almost feel the smirk on Klaus's face.

That was something between Klaus and I...in the last month, he and I spent every day together.

He often smirked when I had an attitude, or when I was brusque or rude...almost as if he enjoyed my little quips.

Kasha, however...was not so amused.

I noticed the smirk leave his face, and his golden gaze suddenly felt even colder than the metal.

"The virtue of a nobleman's daughter is to hold herself—quietly—with poise, grace and dignity, as well as *respect*."

I felt my cheeks burn.

He was telling me I was being shameful, and making my father look bad.

Klaus stirred at my side; a bit agitated.

He could tell that I was…less than enthused about marrying Kasha Fazar.

"You will warm up to me soon enough," Kasha murmured, soft. "For now, I have a gift—" he said, and pulled a box from the back of his horse where it had been strapped into place.

It wasn't a large box, but I assumed that this was the gift he'd mentioned before. I didn't want to be rude, and I knew that my father wanted me to get along with this man, so…I tried my best to smile and act friendly.

"I had noticed you seemed to be quite taken with my horse, and so," he said, opening the box and lifting out the gift.

Inside was a model of a stunning, beautiful, wooden-carved grey horse covered in white speckles all over its body, with a white mane and tail, and white feet made of what felt like fine yarn.

"Wh—"

"It is a model of a horse for your chambers," he smiled. "It is a model of a rare breed from another continent."

"Oh," I said, looking at it. "It is quite beautiful…thank you."

"It was no problem," he told me. "Have you learned to ride, yet?"

"Oh, no," I said. "I haven't gotten to riding lessons, yet."

"Ah, I see. Well, I could show you. I learned to ride when I was five, as it is an important thing in a lord's life. I would be happy to show you."

As much as I disliked the idea, I had to admit that I had nobody else to teach me…and I would love to learn to ride.

Father was so busy with running the city and dealing with the other nobles, my mother was sick, and everyone else was busy working…

Though noblewomen never rode horses in this nation, and never needed to ride…it wouldn't hurt to learn, in case I ever needed it.

"Would you…really teach me?" I asked, feeling hopeful.

He looked vaguely surprised. "Is that really so shocking to you?"

"Well, noblewomen don't usually learn how to ride, as it isn't a common activity for women. And, I suppose, I didn't expect for you to offer."

He shrugged. "It would be a good bonding activity, wouldn't it? We will be getting married in five months, anyway."

I blushed, and I felt uncomfortable when he gave me what others might have perceived as a warm expression…only, I felt like I was sitting in ice.

Why did I always feel this…this unnerving, searing cold from him?

"You could teach me in something, in return? I have a transmitter stone for mana—I have a little mana, though, admittedly, not a lot—and I can cast small, low-mana-cost spells…the problem is, I don't actually know any. I know how to generate a small portion of mana into the transmitter stone, but nothing else. You are from a mage family, your highness, so I am certain you know at least a couple of low-level ones," he said, smiling at me. "Would it be possible to show me a couple of low-mana spells?"

I hesitated. "I, uh…I will need clearance for that," I admitted. "I don't have the authority to make a decision about teaching spells," I said.

I wasn't actually sure if that was true or not…but still, something told me, in my gut, that a non-mage should not be learning spells…

Especially not someone who made me so uncomfortable.

Chapter 6 – Klaus

November, 139 Imperial Year

I watched with a little flustering tingle in my gut as Kasha walked around the courtyard, holding the reigns of his horse as Princess Claudianne sat atop of it.

They had been practicing for a few days, during this third visit of his to the palace. He seemed to come once a month, and the princess seemed especially grateful.

He had intended to come more, but she had told him that she was not allowed to teach him magics.

Honestly, I was glad she'd made that decision, though he seemed…oddly pushy about the issue. He regularly asked her if she truly couldn't bend the rules or sneak a spell in without anyone finding out…

Why did he want to learn magic so badly?

Non-mages didn't need spells…and everyone knew that non-mages were caught up in spell-casting, and often times ended up with serious psychological damage from wanting more and more and more of it.

It drove people mad.

She had a good reason for turning the request down, at least…and I was glad she had followed her gut.

She had actually asked me for my opinion, and I had told her honestly.

She had thanked me by hugging me, and that same warm, peaceful, anchored feeling had returned.

My mana had rushed through me like a weight, a warm weight.

There were no longer any lingering doubts. This girl had something to do with my mana network inside of me, my mana roots...but what?

I needed to know. I needed to talk to Qassim...but would he even tell me anything, if I asked?

It wasn't like I could leave the palace. Once the Grand Duke had reached out to my adopted father and cleared my entrance to the palace with him, and had my things brought from home shortly after my arrival...I had been stuck here.

I hadn't heard not even a peep from Qassim, since.

Had I...been abandoned?

He had never kept it a secret that he supported the royal line, nor that he wanted the princess protected. Had this been his intent all along?

Qassim...was an odd man, sometimes. Things always seemed to work out the way that he intended, for as long as I had known him. Each and every time he set a goal, even if it didn't seem like it would come to fruition...somehow, in the end, it always did.

Every time.

It made no sense, really. Logically, he was one of the luckiest men I'd ever heard of in my lifetime. He was very sneaky about it.

Always hinting at things, playing the cards on the table of every card holder…almost as if he had an eye floating behind each and every player at the table, reading their every move without anyone's noticing it. Then, when he wins, he acts like it was expected all along.

Was he somehow manipulating everything with sorcery? I wouldn't actually put it past him to do so, honestly. I wouldn't be surprised in the slightest to learn that he was.

Qassim was…Qassim.

He was a mystery. A funny, loveable, wise, somehow seemingly-all-knowing mystery.

He had always been that way.

Still, I found it surprising that he hadn't even written me a letter since I'd come here, or shifted into his cat form and come to see me.

"You are a mage too, then?" I heard the young lord ask, vaguely, but I wasn't paying much attention…until he loudly cleared his throat. "Hey! Do you not hear me? Guard!"

"Klaus," I heard my lady call, and I startled, coming back to myself and glancing between them.

"I am sorry, I was lost in thought. I beg your pardon. What is it?"

"You are a mage?" Kasha asked, expectant and a glare of mild irritation on his face.

"I am mage-blooded, but I am more proficient in warrior things rather than sorcery," I told him, trying to get out from beneath his scrutinous gaze. "My family is a sorcery family, but I had weaker mana than they."

He seemed to consider this. "Who is your family?"

"Qassim Malik," I informed. "I am Klaus Malik."

"Ahh, the Malik house. I am shocked to hear that a sorcerer as powerful and well-known as Qassim would have a son who is not proficient in sorcery…"

I shrugged. "It just wasn't something I focused on a lot."

"I was surprised to see that my fiancé had a fellow mage-blooded guard," he mused, smirking. "There are not many mages in this kingdom. The royal family, Qassim's family, and one other are mages…the rest have been driven out. Even Qassim's family has faced their problems, I am sure."

"I wouldn't know. I didn't leave much."

"…Then how is it, exactly, that you met the princess? Qassim gave up palace work almost fifteen years ago…"

"I was running an errand in the bazaar, and heard her crying out for help as would-be kidnappers were making off with her. I stepped in and rescued her—or, tried, at least, to hold them off until more help arrived."

"…That is very brave of you," he said. "I commend you for such bravery, especially given your age. You cannot be older than myself, right? You look young."

"I will be fifteen upon my next birthday, Lord Fazar."

"Ah, I see. Quite young, indeed. And they made you her guard, just like that?" He asked, sneering.

I shrugged again. "I proved myself, whereas her other guards that day hadn't even known she was gone."

He hesitated. "Quite," he quipped out, before turning an intentionally "alluring" smile on her highness. "Would you like to go back inside, now, princess? We've been riding for a while. It should be about time for lunch, yes?"

She sighed, and let him help her down off of the horse.

I almost stepped in when he made a quick squeeze of his hand on her thigh, but she shook him off herself, and shrugged away from him before stepping, quickly, across the courtyard...me at her heels.

The rest of the day passed in a frustrating way—they ate a meal together, before he insisted on walking her back to her chambers.

When we reached her chambers, he did something that neither of us had been prepared for.

He wound his arm around her waist quickly, pulled her in, and delved his head down quickly. Pressing her back into the wall and his lips to hers.

Fury sparked inside of me, raging in my gut, and boiling my blood.

I could feel my mana stirring and rising in response, and I saw his eye cut at me from the side, taking in my response.

As the princess got her bearings about her and started sputtering, shoving against him and shouting against his mouth, he backed up with his hands up in surrender even as I shoved my unsheathed sword between the two of them, stepping between them and acting as a barrier.

"Hm," he said, eyeing me with a look I couldn't read. "...Low mana, hm...?" He murmured, just barely audible.

He turned, waving at us over his shoulder. "It was good to see you, your highness. I will see you again, soon," he said, chuckling as he made his way back through the corridor.

Claudianne shoved her way through her door, shuffling in a few feet before she crumpled to the floor, gasping and sobbing and snotty.

Ugly crying.

I couldn't blame her. He had completely forced that kiss on her with no warning.

"Your highness," I said, a bit timid as I closed the door.

She gaped up at me, eyes continuing to fill with tears faster than they could spill down her cheeks.

"Come here," I said, holding my arms open in welcome. She flung herself forward, sobbing into my chest and trembling. "Shh," I soothed. "It will be—"

"Don't tell me it will be alright!" She sobbed. "I have to…" She started to gag, and held a hand over her mouth as her face turned a bit green…before she flew up to her feet, rushing over to the toilet in her bathroom and emptying all of the contents of her stomach out. "I have to marry that vile man!" She sobbed between retching.

I cringed.

What could I say here?

She was right…I had nothing. I couldn't say anything to soothe her, or ease her pain. There was nothing that I could do. There was nothing that I could say that would make this any better…because the reality was, in just a few more months, she would be marrying this man, and she would be trapped.

"He...he took my first kiss, Klaus!" She sobbed. "If I had to marry him, I wanted to at least kiss someone that I wanted to kiss for my first kiss! I already have to give him my...my body," she said, cringing at the harsh facts.

I glanced to the side as she washed her mouth out, and ate some candies from a bowl on her small night stand table.

"...Then, don't count that as your first kiss," I told her. "You were not a willing participant. You did not consent to that...nor did you reciprocate. Do not count that farce as your first kiss," I told her, rubbing comforting circles on her back.

She lifted her gaze to mine, and her purple eyes swirled with emotion and different shades of purple with her tears. "...Klaus..." She whispered, a pained breath.

I knew something that I could do. Some way that I could offer her comfort, and help her feel better.

"...May I...?" I asked, staring into her eyes with intent.

She gasped, before she glanced at my mouth, and then back to my eyes. She was turning the idea over in her mind, thinking it over...before she nodded, giving consent.

I leaned forward, ever so slowly, and gently pressed my lips to hers.

I heard her sharp intake of breath just as I took my own, and our lips began to press and meld together, moving as one as I licked softly into her mouth.

She wound her hands into my hair, gasping and sighing softly as our lips pushed and pressed one another.

She turned her face to allow me a different angle of access to her mouth.

I moaned as I felt my mana solidifying in me, thickening and gathering in my chest at my center, where mana was stored internally.

Her...she was it.

Claudianne was my mana source, my root, but how could this be?

Mana roots were directly related to you; they were family.

I didn't want to consider what this meant, but I also couldn't deny that I was curious, either.

How were we related?

Most mages never had issues with their roots, because they grew up with their families and their parents to help them solidify the power inside of them before adulthood, when you either completely embossed your mana in your body and were solid...or you died from having no roots.

Mana roots were formed with blood relatives only.

This princess was related to me, and I needed to figure out how and why.

I needed to speak to Qassim.

A few days passed, and I had felt rather strange around the princess, since realizing that we were related…and also realizing how I felt for her.

I realized how I felt for her because she continued to seek me.

She would crack her door when I stood guard outside, her eyes hazed and warm and sparkling at me.

She would talk to me for hours and hours, going on and on…

One day, when her favored handmaiden had made a pass at me—despite that I found her attractive—I wasn't interested in the slightest.

The only one I was interested in…was Princess Claudianne.

She would seek my counsel, she wanted to be around me as much as possible…I caught her staring at me often, and she would blush and her gaze would skitter away.

I felt tingly around her.

Warm and cozy and safe…so safe.

What was this?

There was also another bonus to this. One that I had hardly believed, and still struggled to understand.

In the past, whenever I had managed to gather mana, it rapidly dissipated and emptied from my system. It never stayed in storage, and I struggled to hold onto any of it.

Since our kiss days ago, my mana had not emptied. The mana that had gathered in my core was still there, untouched and ready for use.

She had solidified that mana inside of me.

I had once saved her life, and now, she was saving mine.

I found that I wanted to seek her out, too, and I had for quite some time. Even before she had let me kiss her. The kiss was just an exemplary bonus.

It was the middle of the night, when I began hearing her thrash and sob.

I cracked her door, peeking inside, and noticed her flopping in bed, drenched in sweat and gasping.

I rushed into the room, shutting the door behind me and striding quickly to her bedside.

"Your highness," I called softly, shaking her gently to rouse her. "Princess Claudianne," I beckoned.

Sobs continued coming, and she began to tremble, shoving against me. "N-no! Don't! Don't hurt me…don't kill…don't…don't touch!" She sobbed, shielding her chest.

"Claudianne," I called a bit more firmly by her ear, shaking her, and she cried out into her pillow before she shot up in bed, wide awake.

"…K…Klaus…?" She asked in a whisper, her body shaking violently.

"It is alright, your highness," I told her. "I am here."

"Oh, Klaus," she sobbed, pulling herself closer to me. I sat on the bed, taking her upper body against mine, petting her hair.

"Shh," I soothed. "It is alright, Princess Claudianne, I am here."

"No," she said, shaking. Her face was deathly pale, almost blue. "I…I am scared, Klaus. I am scared," she said. "I…I had a dream that he came to kill my family…! That his father killed my father, and tossed me at his feet and told him he could have my body before…before he killed me off…!"

I startled. "What…?" I asked. "Who?"

"K-Kasha," she sobbed. "I dreamt that he r-ra…raped…before he…"

I pulled her tightly into my grasp, rocking and shushing as I rubbed soothing circles on her back with one hand, patting her head gently with the other.

"Princess," I murmured. "I would never allow that to—"

"He killed you first," she sobbed. "He called you the…the abandoned prince, and he killed you…before he killed everyone else. Even servants in the palace, they…they were in on it. It was a coup!"

I looked deeply into her bright, frightened purple eyes, and I knew that this…

This was no normal dream.

She was mage-blooded…and though untrained, I knew that many mages had the gift of foresight.

This dream was far too horrible and specific to be nothing but a mind's thoughtless, innocent conjuring.

This was deeply specific and particularly dark.

"Have you ever had such a nightmare before?" I asked.

She considered my question for a long time. "I...I once, when I was very young, dreamt of a baby being taken by a woman who had a knife, and was about to be killed...when lightning started flashing in the room, and electricity and fire began to make the woman seize and stop, dropping the baby—but the magician caught him, and took him away."

I suddenly felt like a frog was in my throat, and I ran to the bathroom and began to vomit.

"K-Klaus?" She asked, coming to wipe a cool wet cloth against my forehead.

"I have to...I have to do something really quickly, but I will return shortly, alright?" I asked. She nodded wordlessly, and I rushed out of the room as if being burned alive.

I rushed into my chambers, and pulled out a piece of parchment. I began to write.

"Qassim,

I have found my mana roots...and received some long-abandoned pieces of information. I need for you to come to the palace and explain things to me, and I mean right now. This is no longer one of your games.

Klaus."

I took a deep, soothing breath, folding the paper into the shape of a bird.

Then, I pulled some mana up through my shoulders, down my arms, and to my fingertips, pushing life into the paper, and it flew off into the direction of my father's house in the city.

I felt sick from the drain of my mana, but I would grow used to it soon enough.

Chapter 7 – Klaus

"A bird messenger. Creative, and nicely done. It is good to see you, son, and good to see you use mana and not be about to die," Qassim spoke to me in his cat form before he shifted, stepping into my chambers from the window. "You should be glad it isn't raining and that my windows were open, though."

I chuckled. "I know you often sleep with the windows open. And I knew it wasn't raining. You water your plants with the rain magic at dusk. It is two in the morning."

He smiled. "You have learned well, my son. So, tell me. What can I tell you?"

I was glad that I'd already bit Claudianne goodnight and gotten her back to bed before he'd arrived. She, mercifully, hadn't asked me any questions.

I slowly walked Qassim through Claudianne's nightmares, and he took a deep, shuttering breath.

"Your hunch was right," he told me. "Those…are no ordinary dreams for a twelve-year-old girl, certainly not." He shook his head. "She is experiencing foresight, as you suspected."

"You…you mean—"

"Yes. That is how I found you," he said, glancing at the fireplace roaring with life in the corner of the room. He sighed, meeting my eyes again. "Sit down son. I will tell you."

He began to walk me through it, through his perspective of that fateful night.

He had heard the cries from his laboratory that sat just outside of the palace. Ever since the original Sultan had been killed, along with the Sultana and all of his children—even his concubine—Qassim had taken residence in a small building outside of the palace, in mourning.

When the Sultan's younger brother and his wife began preparations to take over, he had been happy, but cautious. He had suspected another impending tragedy, and didn't want to get too close to the couple.

One day, he had seen the Sultana-to-be…round with child.

She had taken off her cloak for just a moment, and she quickly glanced around to make sure that nobody was around before re-wrapping herself, and rushing back to her chambers.

Qassim had been keeping an eye one the couple, when one night, she had entered her labor.

During the labor and the cries of the young woman…screams of a different kind rang out into the night.

Qassim rushed to find the future sultan and sultana, only to find them fleeing from the palace…

They were captured and taken to the courtyard, when Qassim noticed…there was no baby.

Neither of them was holding a baby, but the sultana-to-be was still gushing blood and birth matter down her legs and soaking her rich gown, but belly...was much flatter than before.

Qassim shifted into his cat form, rushing into the palace with all the speed he could put into his legs, and using his keen cat-hearing to locate the newborn...when he finally heard the baby's cries.

He saw the infant abandoned on the floor, and a maid approaching.

He watched, carefully, observing for a few moments to see what she would do, what her intentions were.

He watched in horror as she lifted the child by a foot, holding him up high and lifting a dagger into the air.

He gaped, shouting out the spell for lightning and fire even as he shifted into his human form.

As the foul woman was struck by lightning and fire, dropping the baby, he caught the baby just in time before he hit the floor...

Glancing around and noticing soldiers rushing through the halls and through the courtyard, Qassim cast a spell of silence and invisibility over himself and the infant...and proceeded to rush out of the palace, even as other maids and soldiers began to scream and shriek out to search the palace for the baby.

He took the baby home, and named him the name that he had once heard the former sultana-to-be murmur to her rounding belly.

"Klaus," I whispered, tears stinging my eyes.

He nodded. "Yes. Your father and mother...they abandoned you when the chaos started, and tried to flee. They were captured and put to death in the courtyard before the coup plotters fled the palace...and I barely managed to save you. I wasn't sure who was or who wasn't on their side, so I took you home. Now, the threat has moved beyond you."

"Then...the *princess*, she's—"

"That's right, she's—" Qassim started.

"She is your cousin," Amir spoke from the door, and we both startled and gaped at him as he clicked the door shut behind me. "Don't worry. I already knew, vaguely, who you were...the silver hair and purple eyes were a dead giveaway, you know, and the fact that you were raised by a man who is loyal only to the imperial blooded family...though, I expected you to be from the eldest, not the middle child," he told me. "I thought the eldest brother would be your father, and that one of his many progeny had just been unaccounted for or missed. For your father to be the *second* son was unexpected. I hadn't been aware that they'd been expecting at all." He sighed. "This also means that Princess Claudianne...is *not* the rightful ruler of the nation. *You are*."

"W-what?" I asked, sputtering. "Are you insane?"

"Does anyone else know who he is?" Qassim asked, tone dark and eyes frightening.

"Yes," Amir admitted. "The Archduke and I both suspected it. He assumed it first, actually. Like me, he thought you were one of the many offspring of the eldest son." He shrugged. "He means you no harm...and neither do I."

"Why haven't either of you said anything...?" I asked.

Amir looked at the floor. "Because I was afraid that if I brought attention to it...we were both afraid that if we said it aloud, you would suddenly come into danger. Both sons of the sultan, both brothers, had wed women who also had mage-blood. It wasn't common knowledge. That is why Claudianne was chosen to be with someone who is not of mage-blood, and someone who is so powerful already on his own, politically. We thought he could help protect her. He has so much support backing him—"

"Are you out of your mind?" I seethed. "She is terrified of him, for good reason. He's already forced a kiss on her, asked her to teach him sorcery for his mana stone, and she…" I sighed, and walked him through her dream.

He startled. "…What…?" He asked, rage burning in his eyes.

"Yes," I said. "We need to keep a close eye on him. I sense something off—"

"You probably feel her emotions, since she is your mana root—"

"Wait, wait, wait, hold on a minute," Amir said, gaping at me. "She…she's your…?"

I nodded. "Yes. Princess Claudianne is my mana root."

"Oh, heavens…this is even more serious than I thought. That means that to stay alive, you will need to remain by her side and have regular physical contact with her until after you come of age, at least."

I looked away. "The princess seems to have felt something, as well, when she hugged me. Not only did my mana solidify when she hugged me, but she also seemed to react."

They both glanced at one another.

"Has the princess ever shown mana ability before Klaus arrived?" Qassim asked.

Amir shook his head. "No. Never. In fact, her mother was quite concerned about her lack of mana when she was young. What if—"

"I suspect that, much like she is his mana root...he may be hers, as well."

"This is very serious," Amir murmured. "She's going to be married in just a few more months! I doubt that Lord Kasha will just allow her to continue hugging and being around Klaus the way that she is able to now, and if he doesn't—"

"Both of us could die," I filled in, crossing my arms.

"That wouldn't matter much to him, though, if his goal is only to become the sultan."

"What do you mean?" I asked.

"If her dreams truly were visions...he could be planning to kill her after they wed, anyway. He only needs to marry her to become the sultan. Once they marry, he will remain sultan even if she were to perish."

My blood ran cold. "He could be intending to get rid of her..."

"Perhaps he wanted to see if she would teach him any spells to see what her mana capabilities were in the first place," Amir surmised. "While there are rules about teaching outsiders magic, if they have proper mana stones that can hold enough power inside of them, it isn't implausible. Mana stones are necessary for non-mages to cast spells and not go mad. Realistically, she could have gotten the clearance to teach him...but she doesn't know much magic, and what she has tried has almost killed her."

"Like your magic did with you," Qassim said, looking to me. "Before you found your mana root, any magic you attempted almost ended your life. Then it is true…she hasn't found her roots before, either. If he wanted to test her ability, he meant to see how well she'd be able to defend herself. I know that the eldest brother had defended himself and his children quite well—it had taken a lot of battling and a lot of foes to take him down," he sighed. "The middle child, your father…he was not concerned about magic. Like you, he preferred physical combat. He never trained much, since he knew his older brother was sultan and he didn't have to do much work. But when the sultan was killed despite having trained so hard, your father started training then."

"It was just…too little, too late," Amir nodded. "So, he knows that the last remaining sibling is on her deathbed, and her only child—Princess Claudianne—has very little mana ability, then."

"He also knew that they were seeking to wed her to someone powerful, politically, and important in the world of non-mages, to help protect her," I said.

"Only, he might not be here to protect her at all," Amir sighed.

"And the culprits, the leaders of coup, were never discovered or captured," I said, rubbing a hand through my hair.

"That is right," Qassim said. "Now that you have discovered, on your own, who you are and your mana roots…you must practice more diligently than ever, and stay close to Claudianne."

"I will," I said.

"Good. Make sure that you do. We don't want another massacre. That tragedy needs to be avoided."

"Yes, sir," I said.

"Amir, you and Klaus need to start surveilling Lord Kasha when he comes to the palace. Spy on him thoroughly, watch his every move. We need to hope to catch him saying or doing something that is severe enough to get him caught as a conspirator, so that we can save the princess…because if he truly is a conspirator, and they manage to get married…it might just be too late."

Amir and I nodded at one another.

"It is decided, then."

December, 139 IY

Lord Kasha was arriving to the royal palace today, and Amir and I had already made a plan.

Qassim would be waiting in animal form, following him around discreetly to spy on him that way…though I wasn't sure what form he would take.

A cat? A lizard? A spider or cobra?

Who knew, with him. I knew that the cat was his favorite, but there were only a handful of cats in the palace to help aid in catching mice. I wasn't entirely sure if the others were recognizable or not to people. Qassim, in cat form, was the same color as his hair.

Were there any cats that looked like his cat form? Or would he stick out?

I shook the thoughts from my mind. Qassim's safety was on himself. It wasn't my responsibility right now.

Amir would be taking over day shifts of guarding Claudianne while I practiced sorcery, trained my body and rested. Then, at night, I would take over and comfort her, letting my mana gather, grow and solidify as I hugged her and she clung to me.

Part of the reason for this was that Kasha needed to not suspect me. Each time I saw him, he would throw unreadable looks at me, and it rose the hairs over my body with how calculative it seemed.

He truly did seem like a villain beneath his... "too perfect" façade.

You could tell it was not his intent to be "too perfect." The truth remained, though, that he was too suave, too perfect, and too pristine to be real.

He was, I would admit, a very good actor...but you could see it in his eyes; something sinister beneath the surface.

He reminded me of a horned desert viper, blending in with and burrowing beneath the sand, ambushing its victims so that it doesn't have to put in any real effort into debilitating them.

Beautiful...but venomous and deadly.

If he was comparable to a horned desert viper, Claudianne would be compared to a delicate grey bunny...with her pretty lavender eyes. She would be easy prey for someone like him.

In the last couple of weeks, Claudianne and I had gotten even closer. She had started having nightmares at least once a week, and grew more and more frightened with each passing day...and she was particularly afraid of his impending monthly visit.

I could only pray that he would reveal something, anything, that we could use against him to get him out of the palace before they were married.

Once he was sultan, he would command the entire palace, and there would be nothing that any of us could do.

We had to catch something before then...we just had to.

There was also the mystery of who had been behind the assassinations of my uncle, the eldest brother and his family…and my father and mother, before they could even be officially coronated.

One thing was certain, in the grand scheme of things; if the conspirator was someone else other than Lord Kasha, they would act either right before the marriage, or immediately after the coronation. There was no way that they would intervene during the coronation itself, with Kasha as the future sultan, if he were involved. There would be no point. He had to have her alive in order to be coronated as the sultan.

My guess was that if he was *not* involved, they would attack right before the wedding, to prevent the marriage and the coronation entirely.

If he was involved, however, they would only attack after the coronation—after he had been named the sultan.

Unfortunately, if the conspirator was Kasha and we didn't manage to get any incriminating evidence before they got married, then there would only be a very small window between the wedding and the coronation for us to do something…because if the wedding took place, that would signal to us that Kasha was somehow involved.

There was no way that a conspirator who was not with Kasha, and who was against a mage-blood royal family, would actually wait for him to marry her, get her pregnant and give birth before they attacked.

What was the point of that? Who would want to wait for that, if their goal was to wipe out all of the mage-bloods?

A matter of a day, at best, if we were lucky.

Those were the two options we were looking at, here, realistically.

I felt my skin crawl, and I glanced at my magic mirror that showed me the courtyard in front of the palace—a new spell I had been working on.

Kasha had arrived to the palace.

Chapter 8 – Claudianne

December, 139 Imperial Year

I trembled as I gave a curtsy, hoping that my fear wasn't too evident.

Even though the only way he had truly offended me was stealing a kiss without my consent, the nightmares that I had only grew more terrible.

It had shifted from him murdering me just after our wedding, to drugging me and raping me before murdering me when he found out that I was pregnant…and the latest, most terrifying nightmare of all—murdering me after drugging me, raping, forcefully impregnating me, and killing me only after I had miscarried a child.

What twelve-year-old girl had nightmares like these…?

I'd barely had a kiss, before Klaus had helped me. I had never been touched beyond that.

Why would I dream of these things?

Each night, when I had nightmares, Klaus prodded and asked me to share them, but the trauma that I felt was only too painful for me to relive it aloud, outside of my own mind…

Klaus grew more and more concerned about me, but wouldn't tell me why he was pushing for me to tell him about the dreams.

Why was he so insistent on knowing?

I couldn't fathom why.

I could tell it; Klaus was hiding something from me.

As I clung to him during the nights, begging and pleading with him not to leave my side and letting myself feel heavy and safe and weighted for the moments that his skin touched mine—as those were the only times I had ever felt that way—he seemed to not want to make eye-contact with me. He acted distant, and it was cruel to me.

I had wanted to grow closer, but I could feel him putting up a wall.

It was odd—part of why I didn't want to tell him about my dreams was because, after that first nightmare and what I had told him...he had started acting more distant and he didn't look at me quite the same.

The affection in his gaze had changed a little...but...

Why?

I couldn't understand it.

Then, he had requested to switch shifts with Amir—to have Amir guard me during the days, while he guarded me only while I slept.

Painful rejection speared me...and I knew how ridiculous it was.

I was to be married in just a few months, and here I was, upset that my palpable affection and feelings for Klaus were pushing him away and that he was rejecting me.

It was forbidden for me to have a secret relationship with him—of course it was. He was my guard. If I decided to bed him, he wouldn't have a choice…but that wouldn't save him from being executed if we were caught, either.

I knew the reality.

We weren't allowed to be together, and so his response to our feelings was to shut me out and avoid me.

I had ruined everything…!

I had wanted him to kiss me that night, but he had initiated it. He had been far too into that kiss, far too much of an active participant, to have been unwilling. There had been way too much feeling in it.

I could see his feelings in his dark, bright violet eyes. I could see that he loved me…

Kasha startled me when he reached out to me, but Amir, thankfully, stepped between us.

"Princess Claudianne has ordered me to restrict any physical contact, Lord Kasha. She does not wish to be touched before the wedding."

He backed up, hands clasping behind his back and a serene smile gracing his lips…but there was a coldness in his eyes that he couldn't cover.

"Of course," he said, voice quipped a little. "My apologies, princess."

I gave another curtsy. "Sh-shall we g-go to have our m-meal?" I asked as steadily as I could, praying that he wouldn't point out my obvious discomfort.

He narrowed his eyes...but he didn't comment on the stuttering, thankfully.

He followed along as we made our way through to the dining hall, and sat down to eat our meal.

I noticed that the maids, in particular, stared at him quite openly and responded to his every whim.

I could tell that he would be highly favored in the palace.

"So," I spoke up. "Should I b-be expecting..." I cleared my throat. "A h-harem...?" I asked.

He glanced up at me, and he held my gaze for a long, long moment, with an odd look on his face.

If I had to name the expression, it would look as if he were saying, "isn't that just a given?"

"...Is that truly any concern of yours?"

My heart dropped. "W-what...?"

"I am fairly certain that every sultan has had a harem, have they not? Isn't that standard procedure? A sultan needs to have many children, after all, especially given your family's...*bloody history*," he sneered. "Perhaps if there are some royal children who are not of mage blood, they may be spared in case there is another dark tragic night, right?"

I could feel the blood drain from my head, and the edges of my vision grew dark.

"Princess?" He asked, though his voice sounded far away.

There was no escape. I would never be free.

I would never be loved.

A Sultana could not have a harem...that is, unless she was widowed by the death of her Sultan, and she had not had children old enough or able to take the throne.

He was right. A sultan almost always had a harem.

There had been only two sultans in our kingdom's history who had refused to do so—the sultan, Claudian Jakard, for whom I was named, had married the princess from the Night-Bringer Kingdom in the West, Vielle Night-Bringer. His foreign Sultana refused to tolerate him having a harem, and he had been so enthralled by her beauty and culture to deny her.

Their eldest son, Claudel, had refused to have a harem, either. He had wed a beautiful mage-blood from the same country as his mother, and he respected her too much to indulge in even owning a harem.

Every other sultan since had ruled over a harem, even if they hadn't really made use of it often.

That had been over a hundred years ago, however, and our history was deeply entrenched in a sultan owning and bedding an abundance of women to ensure that his seed survived and thrived.

It had been the year 027 IY when Claudian had ruled our kingdom. His son, Claudel, had taken over in the year of 043 IY, and ruled until the year of 071 IY.

Since then, it had been the way that it was, now.

My head spun, and the last thing that I saw was Amir rushing to my side, pulling me into his arms with a concerned look on his handsome face, crying out my name...he sounded so far away...

When I awoke, it was dark, and I was in my chambers. I could hear my father speaking in hushed, upset tones nearby.

"Plagued by nightmares, too," I heard Klaus's voice whisper to him.

"Nightmares?"

"Yes, your grace. I suspect that her fear of him has grown to where just being around him is stressful."

"Do you mean to say that these nightmares, they—"

"Yes, I believe they must be, to incite such terror," Amir said. "They seem to be visions…but she won't tell anyone about them."

"Then they must not be so bad." My father's voice was firm and uncompromising. "She is the last chance our kingdom has to be steady and stable under our bloodline."

"But, I—"

"I know what you would mean to say, but it is not plausible. You would face even worse danger. The people wouldn't believe it, and those who did would probably not stay quiet."

Klaus sighed heavily. "Yes, your grace."

"We suspect involvement," Amir said. "We are waiting for anything out of sorts—"

"Leave it alone," my father demanded.

"But, your grace—" Amir and Klaus both said, but my father cut them off.

"I checked into him thoroughly. There was nothing that looked out of sorts, and his family is supporting us...quite heavily. We lost so much support when it was announced that she would become the sultana, and many of our people condemned us for seeking power and not passing the throne on to another reputable household. I...our entire family would be ruined if we lost the support of Kasha Fazar or his father."

Tears stung my eyes behind my closed eyelids, and I struggled not to make any sound.

That was it, then.

This was happening. I was marrying this man. My father didn't care about my feelings.

Our family's livelihood was on the line, and that meant that my livelihood...didn't matter. That was good to know, I supposed.

I took a deep, slow, calming breath through my nose, and I willed my brain to shut down. Slowly, but surely...My feelings...

Turned off.

January, 140 IY

"This fireworks display is quite lovely, isn't it, Princess Claudianne?" Kasha asked, sitting at my side. I nodded, but because I didn't give a verbal response, he turned his attention to me. "Isn't it?"

"...Yes," I pushed myself to answer.

Then, I took a deep, sharp breath, overwhelmed by the energy it had taken to answer, and he glared at me.

"You try my patience with you," he scolded quietly. "Ever since you fainted that night last month, you have barely said two words to me...or to anyone, from what I've heard around the palace. Are you truly that upset over my choosing to have a harem? Because if you are to remain as you are now, I will desperately need the reverie away from this, this...mound of emotionless blob."

I didn't give a response. I didn't feel anything.

In the last month, my father and attendants had all been very concerned, at first—and then, upon my refusal to have a conversation and tell anyone why I was being the way that I was being—they had all just left me alone.

The only two who still actively attempted to reach me were Klaus and Amir...even my best friend, Saffora, had finally given up after a month of my refusing to answer her.

Doing anything that required me getting out of bed—or even speaking—took such a toll on my energy levels and physically exhausted me.

I didn't want to even...be, anymore.

Kasha, during the rest of his visit last month, had thought I was being petty and just throwing a tantrum...but this was his seventh day into his current trip, and he had discovered quickly that this was not a phase, and it was not reserved for just him, either.

He had quickly expressed his irritation over this fact, and his disdain for my sudden behavior change.

Not that it mattered—he had already proposed the marriage, and our official engagement ceremony had been today.

I had been prepared in a nice gown, we had eaten a fantastic meal in front of the entire court, he had presented me with an engagement gift—a horse that looked exactly like the model he had given me before, which I actually had liked. A beautiful stallion, his mane so silky and soft...

Then, there had been fireworks.

We were officially set to marry in two more months, in front of the court. We were officially engaged, and it was full-steam ahead.

There was no longer any backing out of this, unless my father or his father decided upon that themselves. It was no longer up to Kasha or myself.

It was too late.

I knew that my father would not cancel this engagement, and neither would Kasha's father, who sought for his son to become sultan.

All I had to do was remain numb.

I could do this.

I could get through this…and if…

If I died, then…I will have died for the cause, right?

I would have died for the sake of my father, our family name, and the kingdom's happiness and well-being.

That was worth it…wasn't it?

Chapter 9 – Klaus

January, 140 Imperial Year

"Shh," I soothed, stroking her hair.

It was another nightmare in the middle of the night…only, she no longer cried once she awoke.

She just lay there, calming down and getting herself back into her quiet, mentally dormant state.

She had changed so much over the last month that it was hard to fathom that she was even the same person. None of the servants even bothered speaking to her beyond the morning greetings and nightly well-wishes anymore.

She had completely changed.

Not even her new steed made her very happy, and Lord Kasha had been livid over that.

He would regularly approach her servants, inquiring after her, and would scoff and skulk off when they informed him that she was just as silent and non-feeling as she had been before…

"I am here, princess," I told her. She didn't respond. "Are you alright?" I asked. She nodded, silently. I sighed. "Princess, I wish that you wouldn't fold in on yourself this way. This isn't healthy for you. Nobody wishes this for you."

She leveled me with a look that made my skin crawl—a dead, numbed and mildly irritated expression.

It reminded me of a corpse that had died with an agitated expression, or something.

It was eerie, dark, and discomforting.

I knew that her father didn't seem to care about her shift in behavior. If anything, having her this way seemed to placate the situation.

She was no longer fighting the situation anymore.

She had just…given up.

I was desperate to pull her back.

Somehow, someway…but how? How could I bring her back to herself?

February, 140 IY

Her birthday was only three weeks away, now, and she would soon be married to Kasha.

Much to my dismay, as well as Amir's and Qassim's...not even a shred of evidence had come up against Kasha.

It was frustrating and alarming, how well hidden the malice was, but I could plainly see the calculation in his eyes as he eyed my princess, as he talked to her attendants and asked after her...as he asked her father if the wedding was truly going to happen as promised.

Almost as if he expected them to back out...but a knowing expression, smug, would cross his face when he walked away after confirming that the marriage would, indeed, take place.

It was disturbing, and more than a little suspicious.

The day passed uneventfully, according to Amir, but I finally came into her room one night in the middle of February, when she was having another nightmare.

I sat her up, and did my usual, nightly routine—I patted her head, rubbing soothing circles on her back...

Only this time, tears spilled down her cheeks even after she had calmed down.

"Claudianne…" I murmured, taking her face in my hands. "Please…do something. Appeal to your father. It is so hard to see you like this. I will help you every night, if I can, but only you can stop this."

"…I…" Her voice cracked, hoarse from lack of usage, but I waited with baited breath to hear what she would say. I didn't care if it took a whole day for a single sentence. "I…can't stop…this. Not…now…father…will never…" She took a sharp exhale, her body leaning into mine.

I wrapped my arms around her body, giving as much skin-to-skin contact as I could. I knew that she sought it out from her needing her roots.

I was her mana root. Physical contact with me comforted her.

Made her feel at peace.

She took a deep breath, steadying herself and gathering her energy for her next few words. "Father would…never allow it. He…would rather me…die for…our family name. At least…then…he will have…support from…Kasha's…father."

I realized, as it hit me full force, that she had heard that conversation, back on the night that she had fainted in December.

She had awoken and heard part of the conversation, because I specifically remembered her father mentioning that very fact.

"You shouldn't be willing to die just for your family name," I scolded softly, without any firmness. "Claudianne, please…I…I love you. It pains me to see you suffer through this."

She looked at me with wide, glassy eyes. "You…love…me…?" She asked, slow and soft.

"Yes," I said, nodding. "You and I are close friends, aren't we?"

"...Oh," she breathed, and her whole body seemed to droop. "...Friends...yes..."

The way she said it, and the way she was reacting...I would think that she didn't want to be just "friends."

We couldn't be more than friends, though, no matter how deeply I may have felt for her. I had pushed those feelings down as soon as I had realized what they were, and battled them each and every day that I was with her.

It wouldn't end well for either of us if we were caught.

Not to mention, I was technically her cousin, but I had already had feelings for her before that information had been revealed.

Still, I couldn't get carried away. Just kissing her had been one of the highlights of my entire life, and I knew that I could not press farther than that.

I wouldn't be able to forgive myself if my being involved with her ended up hurting her or her future in any way.

I knew, though, that I needed to communicate this with her.

"Princess—"

"Claudianne," she said.

I sighed. "Claudianne...I do have affection for you in a romantic sense...but this...us...it is forbidden. You could get into serious trouble if we grew to be intimate, and I would never forgive myself for putting you in jeopardy. You hold a special place in my heart, and I do love you...that is why I can't let you get hurt. I doubt that your father—or your fiancé, for that matter—would allow you to be with me, if we were discovered. I would rather be with you as your loyal and faithful guard, hopelessly in love with you with no chance of us ever being together, than to risk your safety or to be taken away from you forever."

"So…you would have me…marry Kasha…have his children…watch him have…his harem…while I live…in misery…for the rest…of my life?" She asked.

I cringed, my eyes stinging with tears at the picture of her holding a newborn in her arms, watching her "husband" be intimate with harem girls, with a toddler hanging onto her hip at her side.

"…I wouldn't wish that life upon you, no."

"…Run away with me," she breathed, and I snapped my eyes up to meet hers.

"…What…?"

"Please…" she pleaded. "Take me…run away…we can start a new life…somewhere else."

"Princess, I…"

"Klaus…" she breathed, and pulled me into a kiss. "Please…"

I could feel myself falling, feel myself being lulled into it like a cobra being seduced by a snake charmer.

"…Yes, Princess," I murmured, before taking her lips with my own.

After this, for the next two weeks, she seemed to perk up quite a bit.

Hope returned to the staff, and Kasha sent word that he expected her to be on this good behavior streak when he arrived in tomorrow.

She and I, during the nights, planned our escape.

I would find her in the courtyard's gardens, at midnight—the changing of the guard shift happened then, and we would have a small window to escape the palace, especially with my magic—the day before the wedding, and we would run.

There was a week left until the wedding, and Kasha would be arriving the following day. She would act as if nothing was wrong, and during the day before the wedding, she would make sure she had only what she had to have packed in a small bag, and we would escape that night after she received a day of pampering to prepare her for the wedding the next day.

The plan made sense, it was ready to implement, and we would figure out the rest as we went.

I already had a bag prepared.

March, 140 IY

The day before the wedding arrived, and it seemed to be going just as anticipated.

Everything seemed fine.

She had made one last appeal to her father, the night before, and when he had vehemently refused to cancel the engagement, she had come to me and told me that she had made her final decision; we were doing this.

We would leave.

We would run away, leaving everything else behind.

I had been busy with preparations of my own—I had told Qassim of my plans, and he had actually agreed with them. He agreed that he would help us, even if it was only to buy us time to escape. He was a good man like that.

That night arrived, and I patiently and nervously waited the appointed time.

At ten till midnight, I made my way through the halls to the courtyard's gardens as we had planned…only…

When I arrived, I arrived to something I had not anticipated.

No, there was an ambush.

A hooded and cloaked man stood there, holding the princess in his grasp, and she struggled against him and sobbed, pushing against his hold.

I gasped, unsheathing my sword and rushing him, doing my utmost to fight him without hurting her.

"You're better than I anticipated, but still not good enough," he chuckled, the sound throaty and too happy, considering that he wasn't doing so well. I had already landed a few blows.

"I wouldn't be so cocky, if I were you," I scowled at him, swinging and taking a large slice into his arm.

He just continued to chuckle, mindlessly, even as the princess continued to sob.

"Don't worry, you won't notice yourself losing," he vowed, and the most eerie, discomforting feeling sank into me as my heart dropped to my gut.

Something wasn't right...

"The princess must feel night and tight," he sneered, chortling. "How nice and tight that virgin pussy must—"

I slashed his throat, wincing as my slash caught her shoulder—but he dropped her, and she collapsed to the ground.

As I pulled her into my arms, I gaped openly as the doll flopped like pudding in my hold, and began to melt.

"W-what the—"

"A clay dummy spell, fool," I heard a voice say, before something struck me in the back of the head.

I could feel heat leaving my head as the man ran away, taking the bodies with him...and I used my last bit of strength to send out a signal flare spell—only visible to Qassim, because it was his mana imbued in this mana stone for this very purpose that he had given me as a young child—and then, I fell into darkness.

When I came to, my head throbbed painfully, and I glanced up at Qassim and Amir...who both sat there in utter defeat.

"W...what..."

"Klaus!" Qassim cried, rushing to my side. "Oh, Klaus..."

"What...happened...?"

"My...my trip wire spell caught the mage leaving the palace, but I was focused on trying to figure out what was happening. It...it was too late, by the time I learned."

"...Where is Claudianne?" I asked, trying to sit up.

"She and Kasha married an hour ago," Amir said, his voice dark. "She said she had no choice."

"...What...?" I asked. "But we—"

"I know about your plan. She told me. But you didn't plan for spies."

"Spies?"

He glared at me. "You weren't careful enough!" He shouted, crossing his arms when Qassim waved him off.

"Klaus...Kasha had a mage spying on you for him. He knew of your plans with Claudianne, and...he intercepted you."

"...I...I don't..."

"He made his move. The princess refuses to disclose what happened, but from the physician's report before the ceremony, regarding her virtue—"

"Oh, *fuck*," I whispered.

The Imperial Physician, during the pre-wedding ceremony for a princess or a daughter of a noble marrying another noble, would check her virtue, to ensure she was a virgin bride. If she wasn't, generally, the wedding would be called off…

That is, unless the groom insisted they carry on with the wedding—which was only done if *he* were the one to claim that virtue.

He nodded. "Yes. It…" He took a shuttering breath, trembling. "It is as you suspect."

Tears burned my eyes, and I felt myself falling back into darkness as Qassim began chanting a sleeping spell.

"C-Claudianne…" I murmured.

Chapter 10 – Claudianne

March, 140 Imperial Year

"And where is it, princess, that you think you need to be going so late at night?"

All the hairs on my arms stood at attention, and fear spiked in my heart.

Was this it? Was this where I would die?

Would he kill me for trying to leave?

"Come on, come inside and let's talk about this," he said. He gestured into my chambers, pulling out a jar of chilled fruit tea, from the looks of it. There were chunks of fruit inside of it, but it didn't match the color of regular juice, and it didn't look like alcohol. "I brought this special tea from the West, because I know that your family's roots hail from the continent to the West. I wanted to share a special drink with you before the wedding tomorrow."

"…Is that all?" I asked, trying to smile and calm my heart.

Surely, if I took too long, Klaus would check on me, wouldn't he?

He would make sure that I was safe.

He smiled that odd, "too-perfect" smile of his, and nodded. "Of course. I promise, I just wanted to have a nice moment with you before the wedding tomorrow. I was a bit nervous, you see. I was afraid you might refuse to marry me, and I wanted to make sure you knew that I was just as nervous as you."

His excuse was plausible…and I knew that Klaus would search for me soon, if I didn't show up within a few minutes after our determined time to leave.

I would be safe.

So, I nodded, and invited him into my chambers…quickly and inconspicuously discarding my bag off to the side, when he wasn't looking.

He made his way to the small table, sitting and opening the jar.

Before I could even ponder if it was laced with poison, he drank a giant sip of it right in front of my eyes.

He wouldn't do that if it were poisoned, I imagined.

So, when he passed it to me across the table after I had sat down…I tried to smile pleasantly, and took a good, deep smell of it first—it smelled really, really good.

So, I took a large sip of it.

He took another sip, before passing it back to me, and then told me that I could have the rest of it—I seemed fond of it, and it was a gift, so I should enjoy it.

I had to admit, I loved the fruity taste, and it was tea but it tasted like fruit juice!

It was actually quite nice.

"So, how are you feeling?" He asked about five minutes later…or…

It felt like five minutes, at least.

I needed to go.

"Go?" He asked, and I startled a bit.

Had I said that aloud...?

He smiled softly at me. "You did, actually."

Wait a moment...what...what was going on?

I suddenly felt very sluggish, and time seemed to be passing really fast.

"Oh, that's the effects of what I gave you. This tea was special, you know."

I tried to respond, but I could no longer form a response on my tongue.

"Ah, it is affecting your speech now. That is good. I would have hated to need to wait much longer," he chuckled. "Hah, don't worry, Claudianne—I will take care of you." He took me into his arms, and though the room spun violently as we moved, I felt steady when I was lying on my bed. "This tea will cause you to feel sluggish, and time isn't moving that quickly, in reality. You must be wondering why I am unaffected, but I took an antidote before I arrived. I can drink this tea as much as I wish, and remain oblivious to any changes." He shrugged. "Don't be alarmed—it will wear off in time for the wedding."

I tried to croak out a response, but I only heard a garbled moan.

"You must be wondering, 'why are you doing this?'"

I moaned again.

He chuckled. "Well, the answer is quite simple, really, princess. I learned, from a spy of mine, that you and your guard were planning to flee. He won't be coming to save you, by the way. Don't worry, though—I won't have him killed just yet. He could serve as good motivation for you to behave," he sneered. "But he has been...shall we say...*preoccupied*?" He chuckled again. "Which leaves me time to do this," he said. He ripped my chest wrappings away, baring my chest to his heated, amber-toned gaze. "Ah, yes...these are not bad. I can make do with them," he said.

I tried to pull away, but I couldn't move as his mouth descended onto my chest, biting and grabbing at my breasts.

I felt tears sting my eyes as he latched into one, biting hard enough to break the skin.

"I will mark you so fervently that nobody aside from me will ever desire you," he said.

He pulled out a knife, and made small cuts of the letter of his first name all over my chest, carving it into me.

Sobbing moans left me, and he put a rolled-up cloth into my mouth before tying another around my head, muffling me.

He continued touching my body in a way I had never been touched before, and cutting me along the way, forever marking my flesh as his own.

When he got between my legs, I sobbed as he shoved his mouth into my body...

Then, I forced myself to shut down.

Klaus couldn't save me. In fact, because of me, he had been put into danger.

Kasha had drugged me, and was going to force himself on me…and the drugs wouldn't wear off until the ceremony.

Nobody could save me, now.

He had taken my last hopes away.

So, I retreated into my numbed state; the sweet darkness of peace, the unfeeling void where I allowed myself to float, suspended in time and space.

"Oh, back into the numbed stupid state again, hm? You aren't crying anymore. Ah, well, that's for the better."

I moaned mindlessly as he shoved his way into my body, the pain ripping through me as he broke my barrier, and riding the nonsensical dizziness that made me feel sick with each thrust that made the bed beneath me move and my body flop.

I was sure I would vomit.

"Ah, you're so fucking wet for someone who supposedly isn't enjoying this," he smirked at me. "You are mine. You belong to Kasha Fazar, and tomorrow, I will become Kasha Jakard—the sultan of this kingdom. You shall be my doll of a sultana, and I will own you and the rest of this nation," he roared into my ear, picking up his speed with slaps of flesh sounding in the room…

Until finally, there was a pulsating wetness inside of me, groans uttered from him in a blissful manner.

…Was he finished…?

I almost startled when he struck me across the face. "Don't even try to empty my cum out of your body. Don't try to move. Don't try to flee. You belong to me—for I have marked you as such. If you even attempt to stop the wedding or not show up…I will kill Klaus Malik, and you will never see him again. Understand?"

Then he stood, and left me alone...and I fell into blissful unconsciousness.

The following morning, I awoke feeling heavy and sore all over. My bedsheets felt wet.

My handmaiden, whom I had just started to become close to again, screamed and cried when she saw my pitiful state.

"Don't...don't say anything," I croaked when she helped me out of bed.

I was covered in all manner of bodily fluid.

"But, but princess—"

"Don't say anything," I scowled. "I...have to marry Kasha. I have no choice. My family...we need him. I...I need him," I said, feeling utterly sick as I said it.

She turned pale. "Claud," she murmured. "He...he raped you...didn't he?"

"Don't say anything!" I shouted, grabbing her arm and giving her a desperate look. "It...it won't change anything."

She sobbed as she hugged me.

"I'm so sorry, your highness," she whispered. "So, so sorry."

After a few minutes of comforting me, I asked her to go and check on Klaus.

I wanted to know where he was, if he was safe, what had happened to him…

It wasn't his fault that our plan hadn't worked. Somehow, Kasha had just been a step ahead. Somehow…but how?

I sighed, letting my handmaiden get me prepared.

She dressed me in a shiny, large-sequin scale-mail covered halter top that left my mid-drift bare, and some silky, meshy wrap around my hips and thighs, before she called in the physician.

He had my lay back on the bed, and spread my legs, before he flinched and turned his head away.

"I don't even need to pry that open to tell—you have been heavily deflowered…and Lord Kasha has demanded the ceremony to proceed as planned. As such, I surmise that he was the one who took your virginity?" He asked, and I nodded, hoping my smile didn't look too much like a grimace. "Very well. The wedding will begin shortly." He stood, and left the room.

"Your highness," Saffora murmured.

"Just…get me ready," I whispered. "I am alright, Saf."

She sobbed as she helped me get into my golden-lace-embroidered kaftan gown, and a sheer veil with gold threading.

My hair was left down, hiding some of the carnage from the night before from view.

He truly hadn't taken care with me at all. He had been rough, violent, and volatile with me.

No matter how much he may not have wanted me, I was the daughter of the grand duke and grand duchess, who was formally a princess herself. It wasn't right for me to be treated this way…

Saffora left for a few minutes, before she returned, and told me that she had someone to update me waiting at the door…whom was already vaguely aware of what had happened, apparently.

I dreaded this.

I stepped out into the hallway, and Amir was there, waiting.

"Your highness…" he murmured. "Please…tell me it isn't true," he whispered.

I didn't respond, but as I turned, he must have caught sight of my bruised arm, because he trembled and swore under his breath.

"Klaus…was ambushed last night. He was assaulted by a powerful mage—Qassim said that there were traces of very powerful, advanced magic at the scene that did not match Klaus's mana. He was knocked out and bleeding out when he was found, and he had sent Qassim a distress beacon with his mana. He is still unconscious, right now."

I nodded, tears stinging my eyes.

"I see. Will he…be alright?"

He nodded. "Yes, princess, he will recover. He is with Qassim, now."

I smiled. "Good, then. At least the one whom I love…is safe."

"The one who—?"

Before he could finish, I forced myself to shut down.

I turned my feelings back off.

It was the only manner in which I knew how to cope with what was happening right now.

When he finished asking me his question and looked into my numbed face, he lifted his head and gave a nod, acknowledging my choice.

"I see. I understand, your highness. You will not fight this, then?"

"...He...threatened to kill Klaus. I can't...let that happen. I...am in love with Klaus." I shook my head. "I would rather die...than allow Klaus to be killed...for my namesake. Please, Amir...respect my choice."

He kneeled, bowing and pressing a kiss to the back of my hand.

"I understand, Princess Claudianne. Klaus...is the luckiest man in this kingdom, to have a woman willing to sacrifice herself for her love for him."

I gave him a numbed smile. "Come, then. Let's get this horror show over and done with."

Chapter 11 – Claudianne

It had taken over a week for Klaus to be able to return to his duties.

The injury to the back of his head had cracked the skull, he had been struck so hard, and the physicians were amazed with his endurance and resilience. They especially admired how quickly he was recovering. Despite having an injury that would normally require weeks of recovery, after it was only halfway into the second week, he had returned.

His head still had a bandage wrapped around it, but he didn't look too bad, all things considered.

…I couldn't say the same for myself.

Kasha and I had been coronated as Sultan and Sultana on the day after the wedding.

He had spent the night celebrating by pumping me full of alcohol—which I happily gave myself over to, because I had a feeling he would force himself on me yet again and I didn't want to go through it sober—and I had been right.

He had flipped me on my stomach, propped my rear into the air with pillows beneath my torso, and shoved his way to abandon inside of me, burying to the hilt over and over.

I had groaned into the pillows, willing myself into my numbed darkness, and not fought him, despite feeling nauseated and disgusted.

I knew that if I fought him, he would just drug me.

He'd already proven that to me before.

It had been over within thirty minutes, and he left me sticky and messy to go and enjoy himself in his freshly established bar with his friends, drinking long into the early morning.

The next morning, I had been awakened and made aware that the sultan had not shown up for his duties.

I groggily, painfully got up out of the bed, and wobbled my way to the office, where a stack of paperwork was waiting for me…and I set to work.

I had to get a lot of help from the counselors, and my guards had to physically help me get around…but I managed to get it done.

My father watched on from the doorway for only a short time before he returned to my bedridden mother, to care for her.

Kasha would not show up again until I was getting ready to go to sleep…when he would, yet again, force me to the bed and shove his thick length into me, again and again, grunting obscenities into my ear before leaving me in my chambers while I had to get up and clean myself.

I was left, the following day, to deal with all of the paperwork for running the kingdom on my own, yet again.

Such would be our routine, most days.

This endless cycle seemed to last forever.

That is, of course, until his harem was established after the first week had passed.

Once his harem girls—six of them—had arrived, he only had me once a week.

Thank whoever it was that gave him that idea.

Every day, I took care of the running of the kingdom, while he partied and had fun with his harem girls…and then, once a week, he would find his way into my bed and force himself on me, filling me with his seed until he was tired of me, and would find his way back out of my chambers.

Once Klaus had returned to his duties, it became increasingly hard for me to stomach the routine. Klaus would be waiting outside, fists clenched, and Kasha would just chuckle at him as he left.

Each day felt like a battlefield…and each night, it felt as if Kasha were the one who was winning.

Time passed this way for a while…I wasn't sure how much time had passed.

September, 141 IY

I ripped up out of a nightmare just in time to rush to the bathroom and empty the contents of my stomach.

It had been six months…six months since I had started my cycles.

I hadn't started my first cycle until an entire year after I had gotten married, waking in my bed to blood beneath me…Klaus had burst into the room at my shrieks, but when he had seen what was going on, he had gone to retrieve…a maid…?

She had been surprised, but quickly came to my side to help me. She got me cleaned up, helped to show me what to do. She informed me what was happening, and told me what it meant.

Kasha had been informed right away that I was now a woman, capable of reproduction.

That was when Kasha had truly set to the task of bedding me. He bedded me each and every morning, and I hated it.

It had been eighteen months since Kasha and I had gotten married

At this point in time, he had three harem girls who were already pregnant.

Three of his six harem girls were becoming round with his progeny, while I had remained empty and running on powerful coffee and keeping up with the rule of the kingdom.

I was so tired of it all.

I remembered the announcement of his first child—it had been at a banquet in front of the court five months ago, and he had informed me that if I didn't get pregnant by the time that the child was born, and the child was a boy…then he would name that child the heir to the throne, if my first child—whenever I managed to get pregnant, *if ever*—was not a boy…but…

That was only if I managed to get pregnant within the timeframe of the pregnancy.

I had been keeping close track of my cycles, and I had just skipped my last one for August.

It was time for the one for September, but it hadn't come yet, either.

Not to mention, the only thing that I wanted to eat were apples and peppermint. Anything else, and it made me feel sick.

…*Was I pregnant?*

If I was, would that appease him? Or only incite his fury even further, because he would have a child with me who would be part of me and take over the throne…?

I had to wonder.

I decided, after much toiling over the idea in my mind, that I needed to find the physician.

I set Saffora to the task, and she went to go fetch him.

Klaus waited at my side, fists clenched and jaw tightly clenched shut, when the doctor arrived and checked me over.

"A hearty congratulations, sultana…you are finally going to see the fruits of your labors. You are with child."

A strange, tingling feeling filled my heart…something that I hadn't felt in quite a long time.

Fear, but also a strange warmth in my belly.

A powerful affection.

I cupped my belly, tears spilling down my cheeks.

"Hello, my dear little one," I murmured. "Though your father and I are not well with one another…I will not let that affect my love for you. I will love and care for you, my baby, to my dying breath."

Klaus paced the floor, sending worried glances at me.

I knew what it was that he was afraid of.

I had finally broken down and told him the truth about all of my visions from before I had gotten married…which had firmly stopped once I had actually married Kasha.

It was strange, how it just seemed to cut off so sharply and acutely.

I also felt way more solidness and comfort when I hugged Klaus, now, which was odd.

The feeling was far stronger than before, but none of it made sense.

Why were things changing this way?

I wasn't entirely sure.

I could feel the atmosphere around me changing, the energy in the palace. I knew that Kasha had no use for me beyond letting me run the kingdom myself, and bedding me to breed a child.

Besides that, I didn't really have much of a purpose or a life.

I couldn't even remember the last time I had gone outside and enjoyed the gardens, gotten some fresh air...

I felt so trapped.

"Don't you worry, my child," I murmured, stroking my belly. "All will be well. I love you."

For the first time in a long time, I truly felt feeling...and I couldn't understand why I had such a strange wariness in the pit of my stomach, along with the warm weight that settled over me, knowing that I was the vessel of a new life.

Thankfully, though, that night...Kasha did not show up, nor did he show up the following morning.

I was informed, though, that the announcement of our child had been made to the court, and he had been heavily congratulated.

The only ones whom had congratulated me were the physician, Saffora, Klaus, Amir, and my parents.

I tried to hold my head high, even as the strange glances and glares from the concubines and other servants made me uneasy.

January, 142 IY

I waddled through the corridor to the chambers where my parents stayed. It was the middle of the night, and I had been awoken to the news that my mother was in desperately critical condition.

I arrived to their chambers, only to find my father hunched over my mother's form, sobbing.

The worst fear spiked through me as I hurried to her bedside.

"Darling," mother croaked to me when she saw me, and I took her hand in mine, lifting it to my face. "My sweet…sweet darling."

"M-mother," I murmured, tears rushing down my cheeks.

"Don't…don't you ever…forget…who you are. You…are the daughter…of the princess. You are the niece…of the sultan. The daughter…of the Archduke. You are…Princess Claudianne…Sultana of the Imperial Kingdom of Jakard. You are…my beautiful, darling mage-blood daughter. Don't ever…forget who you are, or where…you come from."

I nodded vigorously. "Yes, mother. I will remember."

"I…love you."

Her eyes closed, and she drifted into sleep.

This was the first that she had been conscious in quite a long time. Months, in fact. She had been stuck in a seemingly endless slumber for so long.

She was so thin. Skin and bones, her cheeks hollow. A small trail of blood dribbled from her lips.

"Doctor...?" I asked, glancing to him as Klaus and Amir stood at my sides.

"She will likely not last the night. She has never been in such dire condition."

I gave a solemn nod. "...Prepare a funeral of grandeur, then, and prepare me some tea. I wish to wait and rest in the gardens. Come and inform me...when she passes."

Then I turned, and waddled out of the room.

I was, according to the physician, likely pregnant since July, since I had missed my cycle for August and September before discovering the pregnancy. That meant that right now, I was about six months along or so. Well into my second trimester, nearing the third.

Kasha had hardly seen me during that time, but he had made it clear that he felt no need to bed me, now that his part had been completed. He said he would return to my side once the baby was born, to name the child, and then leave the nursemaids and myself to our jobs to rear the child...while he continued to play and party in the bar and the harem, and I did all of the work.

Anger rose in me as I made my way out of the palace and into the gardens.

I was Princess Claudianne.

I was the Sultana.

I had gone through unbearably difficult situations, and come out relatively safely.

I had survived.

I was of a powerful mage-blood lineage, and the daughter of a princess and an Archduke.

I had fought to get to where I was peacefully.

I deserved better than this.

I deserved to be loved, cherished, and honored. I deserved the man that I truly wanted, who was still a vigilant force at my side.

I would be fifteen, soon. I had already gone through more than my fair share of trials at my age. I deserved some rest, relaxation, and care.

My mother was right. I needed to remember who I was, where I came from. I couldn't forget my roots.

The maid brought me some tea, and then rushed out of the gardens…which struck me as slightly odd.

I knew that since I had gotten pregnant, most of the servants avoided me. Was it because they no longer wished to serve the maid-blooded sultana, or the mage-blooded prince or princess she carried?

The concubine—the most favored, and the one who had gotten pregnant first—had given birth to a son. The other two concubines whom had been pregnant had given birth to daughters.

Kasha was waiting for me to give birth to name his heir to the throne, so I prayed that it was a boy.

I sipped my tea, and let the breeze wash over me. It was particularly warm, despite being January.

All of a sudden, a few minutes later…sharp, stabbing pains made me cry out, throwing my head back as I screeched.

What…

What was happening…?

Chapter 12 – Klaus

January, 142 Imperial Year

We startled as she suddenly cried out, and we rushed to her side, trying to aid her.

"Go for a doctor!" Amir shouted. "Go get the physician!"

I nodded, rushing through the halls in the palace...but the physician was with the sultana's mother, who was gasping and choking on her on bile and trying to comfort her into her passing.

What...was happening...?

The sultana's mother—my aunt—and the sultana, herself, were both in need of the physician.

I rushed into the room, and the guards rushed to block me, spears out.

"It is the sultana!" I cried. "The sultana is in need of the physician; it seems to be serious! She started screaming out in pain!"

"What?!" The physician said, up to his arms in blood matter and other bodily mess as he tried to help the Archduchess. "But...but I..."

He glanced to the Archduke, who looked back and forth between his wife and me.

"...Go. There is no more to be done here. If Claudianne needs help, then go to her. She is our daughter, and the sultana. Go."

The doctor rushed to get himself at least somewhat cleaned off of mess, before he rushed with me through the hallways and out to the gardens.

Her screams and cries sounded all throughout the courtyard, and she grasped her large belly as she sobbed.

"What's happening?!" She sobbed, clutching her belly.

"The sultana needs to be calmed," the physician said, firm. "As long as she is in hysterics, I won't be able to do much to help. She will have to help me help her."

She began to breathe deep, hearing what he said, and trying to calm herself.

"Do-doctor, please, tell me what's happening. Tell me what's wrong with my—"

"What was in that tea?" I asked, glaring at the cup she'd been drinking from. "We need someone to analyze the tea!"

They all three glanced at the cup, alarmed.

"The maid rushed away after she sat it down. That was not normal. But all of the servants have been avoiding the sultana lately, so we..."

"We were too used to that behavior. We weren't paying enough attention," Amir surmised. "We seem to do nothing but fail."

Another harsh crying shriek rippled through the courtyard, making us all wince, and we helped her to get to her lounging chair.

Thankfully, there was a nice lounging chair in the garden, where she liked to sit and relax before any of this had happened.

She sobbed as she began to struggle, and it took us a moment to realize that she was…pushing?

"W-What's happening?" I asked, startled.

"She's pushing!" Amir said, helping to steady her as she almost toppled over.

"Pushing? But it—"

"She's giving birth!" The doctor said, pushing up her gown and exposing her. "The head is already crowning."

Giving birth?

She was only into her second trimester! Around six and a half months or so in her pregnancy!

It certainly was not time for her to give birth. This made no sense.

She screamed again, bearing down and forcing with all her might…

The doctor rushed to cover his hands with a towel, before he shot his arms forward to catch whatever slid out of her body and cut the cord that was—

The cord that was wrapped around…

Oh, no.

Oh, no, no, no.

Sobs bubbled up out of Amir, and he buried the sultana's face into his chest as he held her.

"I'm so sorry," he whispered.

"I...I don't understand," she whispered, turning her head to look at the baby. "I could feel the baby kicking like crazy, and—and then labor started, and—"

"The baby...is only freshly deceased," the doctor murmured. "The cord must have wrapped around while the baby was panicking. Whatever was in that tea, it...it hurt the baby, and he began to panic and thrash and fight it...and ended up getting strangled."

"...'He...'?" She asked. "You...you said 'he'?"

The doctor nodded. "Yes. Your majesty, you have given birth to a son."

We looked as he wiped off the child, unwrapping the cord, and lifted the child for her to take from him.

He had soft patches of dark, dark grey tufts of hair. His body was still a little underdeveloped, and the skin wasn't quite normal. He was born three months premature, of course, so he wasn't actually ready to enter into the world yet.

"...What can cause this?" I asked. "What sort of drug?"

The doctor cringed as the sultana sobbed into her newborn's lifeless body, but he looked to me. "There are a few poisons that can do this—mixtures of herbs and poisonous plants, even spelled herbs. There is no way to know until the tea is examined and a toxicology report is made—"

"So, you couldn't even bring forth a proper child, could you?" Kasha's voice rang out, and Amir and I whipped around to block her from his sight.

He approached with a group of guards, who all looked down their noses at us.

"A useless mage," he said. "You can't use magic, you are horrible in bed, and now, you can't even give birth to a full-term baby?" He scoffed. "Worthless!" He spat at her.

My entire head began to tingle, and his eye shot to me.

"Do you know why the princess agreed to marry me? Aside from me taking her virtue the night before the wedding as insurance that no other man would want to have her, she did it...to protect you."

I gaped at him. "What?"

He chuckled, a vicious smile of victory creeping up on his lips. "You were heavily injured, remember? I knew how close you two were, and I knew all about your plans to flee the palace and elope! You desired your princess!" He laughed out, manic and deluded sounding. "You actually sought to take the princess and run! But I was one step ahead of you, you see, because I have a better brain than you," he said, tapping his head. He through his arms open wide. "I made sure that she didn't make that appointment, and I didn't even kill you. She has only obeyed me because I promised to kill you if she refused."

Anger boiled in my veins, and I could feel the mana in me rising.

"Oh, you may as well stop that," he smiled. "You wouldn't want the princess's efforts to all be in vain, would you? Goodness, I would hope not. You should love her more than that."

He walked up to me and gave me a light slap on the cheek.

"Don't worry, Klaus Malik. I won't hurt the sultana. I need her."

Then, he strode over to her, and inspected the scene.

"What a mess," he chuckled. "It is too bad—the prince seems to favor me more than you. Oh, well," he shrugged. "The prince brought forth by my concubine shall be named Crowned Prince," he declared, and the guards and servants who had gathered around us all clapped and cheered.

Amir rushed to cover the sultana, realizing her state of undress, and the physician reached to take the glass of tea…but Kasha reached it first.

He dumped out the tea into the sand, and kicked the sand away…so we couldn't even autopsy the contents.

Then, he tossed the cup to let it shatter on the stones of the courtyard before kicking the shards into the sand off to the side…affectively removing any trace of liquid, and any trace of poison along with it.

He was right…he truly was a step ahead of us, the entire time.

He shrugged. "Clean this mess up, and keep her out of my sight. Now that I have an heir, I will not be coming to see you. I did my part—it is no longer my problem that you couldn't see it through and produce proper results." Then he turned, strutting away, while Claudianne quietly sobbed into her son's tiny, lifeless body.

Her father gaped openly at us as he stepped into the garden, eyes wide and tears welling in them.

"Claudianne…?"

He came to her side, and immediately seemed to realize what was happening. He wrapped her in his arms, and quietly cried along with her.

We would learn, later that morning, that the Archduchess had passed at almost the exact same time that the prince had been miscarried.

They would be wrapped and prepared for burial by Amir, Qassim, the Archduke, Saffora and myself...since nobody else in the palace would help.

Then, we would carry them out to the grave that had already been prepared for the sultana's mother, as she had instructed, and the prince would be buried with his grandmother.

March, 142 IY

The princess was turning fifteen, but there was no celebration. Only her father and Saffora came to visit her.

She had lost all support, while Kasha only seemed to grow in power and influence.

Another of his concubines had given birth to a son, and so his line was well secured in the crowned prince and his other children.

Claudianne had lost all hope. She didn't even try to get out of bed unless she had to. All of the paperwork she had to do was brought from the office to her personal bedchambers, and she isolated herself there.

Qassim, Amir and I had still not caught wind of Kasha saying much that would incriminate him enough to be dethroned.

So far, he had not actually been implicated in any crimes, and he was very careful about what he said.

There had, however, been quite a number of soldiers arriving from his father's duchy, and his influence continued to grow.

I didn't know where we would go from here.

"There is one option," Qassim told me one day, when I went to his house to visit him.

He made sure to spell the entire home with privacy spells, to ensure nobody would be listening, and we checked to make sure that they worked.

"What is it?" I asked.

"Write to the West," he said. "You are the true prince, Klaus. If you journeyed for the West, and arrived as a prince for this kingdom in dire need of aid—explained the situation—we still have a peace treaty with their empire. You are a direct descendent of one of their royal family members. They are still an ally. We have never made use of that alliance, but two separate sultanas came from that very same kingdom. Surely, that has to mean something. Journey there as a prince, under distress, and explain the situation. Their empire—which is at least five times the size of our kingdom—would surely be able to help us."

I considered this. "But...who would help teach and protect Claudianne while I go?" I asked, concerned. "I had already decided to start teaching her, and helping her learn to use her mana."

He thought on that. "I will," he said. "She knows me. I am the best sorcerer in this country. I will be able to keep her safe and teach her."

"It is settled, then," I said, nodding. "There is just something that I have to do first."

I returned to the palace in my cat form, and trotted up to her and jumped into her lap.

She smiled, snuggling me. She knew my cat form, now.

"Klaus," she murmured into my fur. "My sweet kitty."

I purred into her, butting my head into her cheek affectionately, before I stretched out and shifted into my human form.

"I have something to discuss with you, Claudianne," I said, stroking her cheek...

Only, instead of nodding or answering, she leaned into my touch.

Her hand slipped up my hip, and beneath my tunic, and I gasped as her fingers grazed one of my nipples.

"C-Claudianne..." I whispered.

"Please," she whimpered...and then, her lips were on mine.

I gasped, taking her face into my hands and pulling back, looking into her eyes that burned with longing.

"You..."

"I want to be touched," she breathed. "Loved...cherished. For once, I want to be special..."

I couldn't deny her, and damn it all, I didn't want to.

She was right. She needed this...and so did I.

I touched her softly, tenderly, and let my lips descend over her scarred flesh.

I was still sickened that he had marred her body in such a way, but she was still just as beautiful to me.

I kissed and licked over her flesh, and her throaty gasps and moans as she thrust her breasts up into my face were blissful.

I stroked my fingers over her waist, her torso, her lower belly, her thighs, even as my lips followed that trail with hot, passionate kisses.

Then I spread her wide for me and used my tongue to lick up into her body, loving the way she trembled violently and grasped my hair for dear life.

Since that altercation with Kasha, my hair had actually lightened even more, and now was more white than silvery grey. I had gathered so much mana that it had pushed me more into my mage-blood.

Her fingers clung to the strands of my white and peppery silver hair, even as I buried my jaw in her folds, my tongue flicking over the nub between them.

I could feel her clamping down on my fingers, and just as she began to flutter and her breathing sharpened...I stopped.

She whined, and I crawled up her body and slid my cock inside of her in one languid, fluid stroke.

She came over me as soon as I hit her womb, and she thrashed and fluttered over my virgin cock.

I trembled, thrusting a few times and trying my best to hold out despite how new it was.

"C-cum inside me," she whispered. "I know you're close. I want you, Klaus," she murmured into my ear.

The siren's call if I'd ever heard it, beckoning me to obey...

So, obey I did.

My body immediately obeyed my sultana.

I began seizing as I curled over her, even as my cock spurted my seed up into her waiting womb, buried deep in her pelvis.

It hadn't lasted long…but it was the most blissful, peaceful thing I'd ever felt.

I felt…whole.

She wrapped her arms around me.

"You're leaving, aren't you?" She asked, and I gaped at her. "I can see it in your eyes. You're leaving me."

"Not permanently," I murmured in her ear. "I am going to get help. I will return for you, and save our home. And then, you will rule as a *proper sultana*, and I…I will become your sultan, and you will become my sultana."

She trembled, and the fluttering made me swell again.

She gave a breathy chuckle.

"Make love to me again, Klaus."

"Yes…my sultana."

Chapter 13 – Klaus

April, 142 Imperial Year

I stepped off of the ship and onto the docks, thankful to at last be off of the sea.

It had been a long, month-long journey to the Western Empire, but I had finally reached it.

I had sent a letter ahead of time, and surprisingly enough, it seemed that my message had arrived safely—there were a team of guards waiting there at the dock, ready for my arrival.

At the head of the column, a man with rich red hair, dark tanned skin, and bright golden eyes bowed.

"Welcome, Prince Klaus of the Jakard Kingdom," he said, bowing respectfully. "His majesty, Emperor Ciel Ember Twilight, has instructed us to receive you and bring you to the palace straight away." He bowed again. "Come with us, please."

I followed him and the group of knights got around me, acting as a shield, almost, as we made our way through the town and upward toward the large palace on the cliffside.

I had thought that the Night-Bringer family or Day-Giver family would be ruling, but had I been incorrect?

Was this still an allied nation? Would they help us?

I felt a lump in my throat as we reached the palace, and everyone stopped what they were doing and looked at us in surprise.

Most of them were light-skinned in comparison to me, but there were a handful as dark or darker than I was.

They had such varying appearances, all of them.

We entered the main palace, and stepped through a foyer and some corridors of richly decorated areas before we reached a large, white-marbled space with a throne in the center, a backsplash of beautiful stained-glass behind the throne, illuminating it.

It was...stunning.

It made our kingdom's palace pale in comparison.

This truly was an empire.

There, seated on the throne, was a beautiful man. That was the only way that I could describe him.

He had ash-toned, dark silvery grey hair that looked like dark billowing smoke, and bright, orange-toned eyes that reminded me of burning embers. His skin was a rich, bronzy tan, a stark contrast to his hair and eyes.

"Greetings, Prince Klaus of the Jakard kingdom to the middle east, an old ally of our empire. We welcome you with heartiness and joy. Your letter did not detail much other than that you were in dire need, and so...how might I assist you?"

I took a deep, steadying breath.

I had to get help. I had to get help for my love.

"Your majesty," I said, bowing. "I implore you, as an ally and a desperate man who is seeking to save his love and his kingdom...please, help us."

His expression turned serious, and he leaned forward, hands clasped, elbows on his knees, listening intently.

"Go on."

"My uncle, eldest son of the former sultan, and his entire family were killed in the night by anti-mage faction rogues. The middle son—my father—was about to assume the throne and he and my mother were killed. Luckily, they hid me away, and I was hidden within a mage family in the city. Most of the city...is still unaware of my identity. Only a handful of high-up officials know the truth. The youngest child, the daughter, married the Archduke, and together, had a daughter...who became the next appointed heir to the throne. To receive the throne, they married her off to the son of a duke. This son has been labeled as a suspect, being part of the anti-mage faction, but they have been unable to actually catch him with enough to detain him. He has drugged my cousin—my sultana," I said with affection, and I noticed his head turn a bit. "I am her personal guardian. She and I...we love one another. I didn't discover the truth behind my origins until after we had formed a bond."

"I see," he said, nodding. "Continue."

"The new sultan...has drugged her, raped her, abused her, and even dosed her with a poison to cause her to miscarry their son...but somehow, he managed to erase the evidence, despite that we witnessed it. Without the evidence being brought before the counselors and the court, they won't believe us. They say that we are simply too sensitive toward the sultana."

He nodded. "They can't prove it because he erases the evidence beforehand?"

I nodded. "Yes. And so, the sultan has been bringing in his own army and gradually seizing control of the palace. Before they married, Claudianne—the sultana, and also a mage-blood—began having visions. Visions of the future, confirmed by my adopted father, the palace sorcerer who is the most renowned sorcerer in the kingdom, Qassim Malik. But we were promptly ignored. I wish to rescue her before another tragedy occurs, and before he decides to kill her off."

He hesitated. "How many mage-bloods remain in your kingdom?" He asked.

I calculated that. "Including me, my adopted father and his children, the sultana, and a dark mage who tried to kill me...probably seven?"

"Seven?" He gaped at me, standing. Everyone in the room bowed, and I lowered my head for a moment before meeting his eyes again. "Less than ten? How is this possible? Your kingdom once flourished with mages."

I cringed. "Yes...It did. No longer, however, since the anti-mage faction began using mana-stones, half-baked spells, dark magic, and magical devices to kill us. They always attack in unconventional methods; during the night when we're sleeping, out in the middle of nowhere when we're traveling, poisoning us at tea-times through moles planted as servants in our own homes..."

"I see. And so, why should I help a kingdom of mages who cannot even protect themselves? Why should I help you?"

"Please," I said, lowering to my knees and bowing. "As a fellow mage." I met his eyes, and he looked at me in surprise.

"...You can tell I'm a mage?"

I nodded. "I could feel your mana rising, even as I described the situation to you. Your hair is a little darker than most mages, but I can tell."

He chuckled. "You are the first to ever tell me that you can feel my mana, or that you could tell that I was a mage despite looking like a hybrid or non-mage. Most people see my dark gray hair and assume that I am mixed or that I have no mage-blood. Yet you knew."

I nodded. "Yes, your majesty."

He sat back down, and leaned back, arms crossed over his chest. "I cannot, in good conscious as a mage—and an ally—watch a kingdom whom my mother came from suffer."

I gaped up at him. "P-pardon...?"

He smiled at me. "You may not be aware of this, given that you were hidden away...but your kingdom and my empire have continued to remain on good terms, and have continued keeping up marriage alliances. My mother...is the sister of Qassim Malik."

I gasped. "Then you..."

"As soon as you said that you were the adopted son of Qassim, I knew that I would help you," he smirked at me. "I suppose that I am your adopted cousin, then," he chuckled. "We are family, even beyond the fact that you and I are both descended from members of this royal family. Your ancestor was a princess from this kingdom, after all, and her son also married a woman from this kingdom. Common ancestors aside, now your adopted father turns out to be the brother of my mother?"

"That...that's why Qassim sent me here to seek help...!"

"That is the most likely reason," he nodded. "I have made my decision." He stood. "I, Ciel Ember Twilight, hereby decree that we recognize no other sultan than Klaus Malik Jakard!" He said, and everyone in the room bowed. "Furthermore, we will take our army and journey to the Jakard Imperial Kingdom, and take back the throne for my cousin, whom I recognize as my legitimate relative. My mother has never had anything but love and affection for her older brother, and has made mention of missing him many times. If you are the son that my uncle adopted...then you are my cousin." He nodded, stood, and came to stand in front of me, arm outstretched. "Take the night to rest, cousin—for we will set sail at dawn."

"T-thank you, your majesty."

"Please," he smiled. "'Cousin,' or 'Ciel' will work just fine. We are family."

Then, shocking me, he pulled me into a hug, before walking me through the palace to meet his parents...and my adopted aunt, who proceeded to gush over me and hug and kiss me all over my face.

May, 142 IY

It was a good journey back to the kingdom, albeit a bit worrying.

I was worried about Claudianne.

During the journey, I had spent a lot of time talking to Ciel. Learning about him, his upbringing, the lifestyles and customs of the Western Empire.

His grandmother had been the last named "Night-Bringer", and they had drastically changed the system so that she didn't have to exert herself bringing the night because she was in very poor health. She had died after birthing only one son, and that man had, in mourning of his mother, cast away the Day-Giver and Night-Bringer names.

He took on the name "Twilight," because of his black hair and navy eyes...and then, he had chosen to marry a mage from our kingdom, because he had wanted something different.

He wanted something he hadn't seen before.

None of the court ladies or noblewomen of the empire had suited his tastes, and he had remembered the alliances of our kingdom to their empire through the generations.

He had reached out to the palace, and requested a list of suitable noblewomen and their portraits be sent for him to look over...and the highest-leveled female mage, Qassim's younger sister, had been chosen.

Seeing his mother in person, he favored her more than his father, really.

He had not been their only child, but just the oldest of four sons and a daughter.

I also talked to Ciel about my upbringing, telling him all about Qassim and life as a withering noble family, since we had lost much status since he had fled the palace.

I told him about Claudianne, and finding out that she was my mana root, and I was hers, about how I had slowly fallen in love with her over time...

I told him all about what Kasha was like, how Kasha had found out about our plan to run away, and had intervened and forced himself on her—Ciel had needed help cooling down his raging mana for that one—and about how Kasha had forced her to miscarry their child, naming one of his concubine's children as the heir.

"I would have sought help, too," he said, nodding. "There isn't enough man-power to help you do it alone."

"There is only one question that I have, Emperor Ciel," I said, and he looked at me. "What...is your price...for helping us?"

He smiled. "Well, I will admit...I am intrigued by the idea of finding a bride in your kingdom. My mother has been pushing me to marry, you see, since I recently ascended the throne, and I have yet to find an empress. Perhaps I will be able to find a noblewoman in your kingdom who suits my taste. I would like a woman who comes from the same kingdom as my mother."

For some reason...Saffora instantly came to mind.

"I know of one, whom has stood by my sultana through everything—she almost gave up, when my sultana gave up, but she came back strong and has stuck it out—and she is a beauty."

"Oh?" He grinned at me. "Tell me more."

"She is the daughter of a high-leveled noble, and she serves the sultana as a handmaiden."

I went on to tell him about her looks, and her age and disposition, and by the end, he was already quite interested.

"Yes, I think I shall need to meet this 'Saffora' and find out for myself," He grinned. "Thank you, cousin."

"Thank you," I smiled.

We arrived in the port later that afternoon, and I took a deep, deep breath.

"Now...how do we do this?" I asked him.

"Call Qassim here...we shall consult with him."

I nodded, and sent out a mana flare.

We waited for about an hour, before my father arrived to the docks, gaping at the number of ships that rested in the bay.

"You...you succeeded," he said, gaping out and approaching us. "Is...is this—?"

"This is Ciel Ember Twilight—your nephew, and the emperor of the Western Empire."

He gaped at him, even as Ciel looked over him with interest.

"So, you are my uncle," he grinned, and pulled him into a hug. "Mother has had nothing but affection and love for you in all of her tales of your childhood, growing up. She misses you dearly."

Qassim teared up. "I have a nephew," he smiled, laughing.

"You have several, and a niece, too," Ciel said. "But we don't have time for that right now. We need an update on the situation."

He instantly flinched, hardening. "It isn't good," he said. "Claudianne...started fighting back."

"...What...?" I asked. "Is she alive?" I asked darkly.

He nodded. "She is alive...but she is imprisoned in the dungeons. She fought against Kasha when he tried to force her to..." he cleared his throat. "And, she attempted to poison his head concubine, after the concubine humiliated her in front of the court for miscarrying the prince."

I gaped at him. "What...?"

He sighed. "It is also...he also revealed to us, by accident, that her behavior and refusal of him was why he was feeding her Mane-Lock."

"What?" I raged, trembling with the force of my anger.

Mane-Lock was a poisonous herb that gradually locked away someone's mana, and made it useless. When she came of age, if the plant wasn't filtered out of her system and her mana root filtered in to solidify her mana...she would die.

It was a death sentence, and an excruciatingly slow and painful one, at that.

It was cruelty beyond cruel.

"We need to hurry," he said. "You…brought an army?"

Ciel nodded. "Long time allies, with common ancestors, and with your connection to my mother…we are family."

"Family," Qassim nodded.

"To family," I said, looking up toward the palace.

"Let's go," Ciel smiled darkly.

Chapter 14 – Claudianne

May, 142 Imperial Year

I had been two and a half months since Klaus had left for help…and I was wondering if I would ever see him again.

I didn't know how long the journey took to reach the Western Empire, but surely, he would have sent word by now, somehow…right?

A letter?

A signal?

Something…anything.

I had been locked in the dungeon with little food for a month, now…and I felt so empty.

So cold.

Lifeless.

I was a lost cause, now. Was I even titled as the sultana, anymore? I couldn't imagine that I was.

I had been woken in the night to the drunken sultan in my bed, trying to force himself on me while cursing my lover, Klaus, for my loving him instead of Kasha—and I had screamed.

I was crying out and thrashing, refusing him, and struck him over the head with a candlestick holder.

Amir rushed in, yanking him off of me, when the other guards rushed in and took him into custody, beating him for daring to lay a hand on the sultan. I had not seen Amir again until he had come to see me after I had already been arrested, a month later.

After Amir had been taken, the sultan had left me be, going to the concubines to complain of his woes.

At the banquet three weeks later, the concubines had decided to humiliate me, mocking me and throwing my miscarriage up in my face, even mocking the deceased infant prince who was "too worthless to even take his first breaths."

I had cried and cried, rushing off to my chambers and begging the heavens to let Klaus return.

Only a week later, I was finding myself in handcuffs, being dragged out of my chambers in chains, with the guards and maids swearing at me and condemning me for daring to harm the mother of the crowned prince.

My father was fighting against the guards, insisting that I would never have done this, that I was innocent—to bring forward definitive proof.

His cries fell upon deaf ears.

She'd had her maid, I discovered through Saffora later, dose her with a small amount of poison—just enough to get sick—to frame me, so that I would get in trouble.

Then, the maid had disappeared, never to be heard from again.

Saffora only knew because she'd heard the concubine bragging about it to the other concubines, since Saffora had been transferred to being their handmaiden as further humiliation to me. Taking my own handmaiden, losing my only friend...

After I had been framed for trying to poison the head concubine by one of the concubine's maids, I had been thrown in here after a lashing.

Those twenty lashes had not been too terrible, compared to them branding my right hand and ripping off my fingernails, however.

They had tortured me.

Losing my handmaiden, twenty lashes with a whip, branding my hand, and ripping off all of my fingernails for harming the mother of the crowned prince...a mere concubine.

I had barely been able to look at Amir when he had visited me in prison shortly after my arrest...I was too ashamed.

I looked out of the small barred window, peaking at the full moon in the sky.

When would this end?

I was so hungry and cold...

I startled when I suddenly heard a giant explosion, and I felt the bars of my cell vibrate minutely.

What was happening?

I could suddenly hear a roar outside; voices, what shouted like war-shouts.

I could hear clinging swords, and I saw bright flashes of light.

Cracks of lightning and shots of fire, screams in the night.

Was the palace…under attack?

Had Kasha finally brought war to the palace?

Was he killing my father?

Tears filled my eyes. I was in no position to be worrying about others right now, and yet, here I was, more concerned for my father and Saffora and Amir than I was for my own safety.

Would they be alright?

Would they escape in time?

Should I just…end my own life, now, before they reached the dungeons to finish off the remaining mage-blooded former sultana?

My visions…had seemed to come true, after all.

I glanced around, wondering if there was anything that I could use to kill myself in this cell.

There were stones…could I bash my head in hard enough to kill myself?

There were rafters above me, and chains that I had been brought here in…perhaps I could hang myself, instead, but how would I get the chains up in the rafters?

There weren't really any other options.

There was a dirty toilet in the corner…could I perhaps drown myself?

No…no, I would rather not stick my head in there…

I sighed, taking the chains in my hands…and I began throwing them up at the rafter boards, trying to get them to loop.

Perhaps this was something I should have done long ago.

Klaus wouldn't have been hurt because of me. Amir wouldn't have been hurt because of me.

Father wouldn't have been shamed because of me.

I wouldn't have failed to carry my sweet prince to term.

None of these atrocities would have happened if I had just died a long, long time ago, right?

I finally managed to get the chain to land on one of the rafters, and I shimmied the part that I was holding to bring down the other side.

I tried my best to tie it, securing it, and I managed to get a noose made...sort of.

As soon as I put it around my throat and jumped off of the toilet, however, the chain came undone, and I plummeted to the floor with a hard thump.

I sobbed, rubbing my sore bottom, and tried again...to no avail.

I really was useless.

Useless as the Archduke's daughter. Useless as a mage. Useless as the princess. Useless as the sultana.

Useless as a mother...

I began to sob quietly, pulling myself into the corner and huddling in on myself, wrapping my arms around my knees.

All I had managed to do was bruise my body and my neck and waste my time.

I began to pray. I prayed to whomever would hear me.

"Please…help me escape from here. Let me be freed. If I have to, I will flee the country. I will never return. I'll spent my life in repentance for being worthless. Just…please…"

I wasn't sure how much time that I spent waiting after that.

The noises and screams and magic kept going outside.

It was light outside by the time things started to quiet down, and I blearily opened my eyes to see the sun high in the sky once it was fully quiet.

…How long had it been?

How long had the fighting been going for?

For that matter, how long since it had stopped? I had gotten accustomed to it, at one point, and managed to somewhat sleep.

If I was going to be executed, I at least wanted a little bit of rest first.

There was a certain peace in knowing that my life was about to end.

I was surprised by how long it had taken. I had thought that there weren't many people on our side in the palace, but perhaps there had been more than I had thought. Or had Qassim recruited some help?

Had there been clay soldiers made from magic?

...Would they come to take me out for my execution, now?

I cringed when I heard the door to the dungeons open, and light flickered in when two guards came with torches...

Then, I saw faces I didn't expect.

"Father...? Amir?"

"It is time," my father said, a somewhat strange expression on his face.

Was I really about to die? Were they allowing me this time in order to say goodbye, as a final act of favor for their unwanted sultana?

I couldn't be sure.

The guards opened my cell, and Amir and my father came to my side, helping me to stand.

"W...wha..." I croaked, but I couldn't ask the question.

"You'll see," father said, a somber smile on his face...

He was smiling, but looked sad, too.

What was going on?

We made our way through corridors that were once so ornately decorated and stunning, but were now scarred with scratches, cracks, blood matter...

I cringed, but we continued on.

We made our way out into the raised courtyard that overlooked the rest of the city, and I gaped at the back...

His back.

He was back, standing side-by-side with a man with dark, dark gray hair whom I didn't recognize.

Kasha was on his knees, a cloth tied around his mouth—gagged and chained. Qassim stood on his other side

The man that I didn't recognize spoke.

"The sultana is not the legitimate heir to the throne! Therefore, she is deposed. There is another heir who had a stake to the claim over the throne that was above Princess Claudianne's claim. That is why *this man*, Kasha Fazar, whom drugged, assaulted, raped, and imprisoned the princess—the woman who made him the sultan in the first place—is hereby dethroned along with her. He has committed treason!"

The crowd looked around, murmurs and whispers among them.

"Your kingdom, which has a long and rich history of alliance with my empire, was once one of the healthiest, richest kingdoms known in the world. My ancestor, the Empress Katariah Day-Giver, invited Crowned Prince Claudian to her Empire, and even allowed him to marry the princess, Vielle Night-Bringer. Their son, Claudel, married yet another noblewoman from this kingdom. My mother is the sister of your most well-known, world-renowned palace sorcerer, Qassim Malik. Mage-bloods and Knight-Borns are both heavily integrated in both of our rich cultures. It is time for things to be made right."

Klaus kneeled.

"I name this man—this *prince by birth*, whom has been hiding under your noses all along; the son of the second son and his wife who were murdered just before they became the sultan and sultana—Klaus Malik Jakard, the Sultan."

Gasps from the crowds below sounded, and the servants that were around us who remained—those who had been loyal to my family, I supposed—gasped, looking around in surprise.

I joined them, completely blindsided by this new information. Why had I never known this? How many people were aware of this information? Did my father know?

The man continued. "From this point forward, no longer is he a hidden prince—he is the *rightful heir* to the throne. The throne passed to Claudianne Jakard out of the right of succession, and therefore, she is no longer the legitimate sultana, and Kasha Fazar Jakard is no legitimate sultan. The anti-mage faction army has been defeated. It is time to put this kingdom back in its rightful place."

The booming roar of applause was overwhelming, but I was focused on Klaus.

My heart dropped to my feet, and I felt like I'd vomit.

All of this time, I had wondered why we looked so similar. I had wondered why I felt such a connection to him, why we were so bonded...why he seemed to steady my mana.

All of this time, he had been the true crowned prince, and we'd never known.

All of the time, he had been the rightful heir...not me.

I had taken the throne from him. Unknowingly, but still.

My uncle, the eldest, was sultan. He and his sultana, his concubine and all of their children were killed.

My uncle, the middle child, was about to be the sultan with his wife, but apparently, they'd had a child...who had been hidden all along...?

My cousin, it turned out.

Klaus. The rightful heir. Raised by Qassim, in safe-keeping all along.

He had been the legitimate heir, next in line, over even my mother, because she had married the Archduke and had a daughter.

All I had gone through...all of it had been for nothing, it turned out. I had suffered for nothing.

I had been an illegitimate sultana, all for nothing.

I needed time to cope with this.

I dropped to my knees, and they finally turned my attention onto me.

I startled when Klaus—looking more beautiful and radiant than I had ever seen, donned in royal armor and splattered with blood from his enemies—helped me to stand.

His white hair was bright in the sun, the silver strands shining brilliantly like embroidery in his hair. The blood splatter all over him gave him an ethereal look...he looked like a red rose, to me.

A single red rose.

Beautiful. Perfect. Sublime. So mighty in its delicate twists.

The petals soft but the thorns stabbing all who approach.

Beautiful, but full of sting.

He took my hands in his own.

"Have you waited for me, Claudianne? Will you still allow me to be yours, and you to be mine?"

"...What...?" I breathed.

He chuckled. "I named you my sultana before I left...remember?"

I startled in his embrace, the memory sudden and sharp in my mind, vivid as if I were reliving it.

"You're leaving, aren't you?" I had asked after he had shot his seed into my body, and he gaped at me. "I can see it in your eyes. You're leaving me."

"Not permanently," he murmured in my ear. "I am going to get help. I will return for you, and save our home. And then, you will rule as a proper sultana, and I...I will become your sultan, and you will become my sultana."

I had trembled, and I had felt his cock harden inside of me again.

I had given a breathy chuckle, amused by how eager he was.

He may not have been my first...but I was his.

I was his. I knew that I was...I gave myself, my heart, to him...then and there in that moment.

"Make love to me again, Klaus."

"Yes...my sultana."

I gaped at him. "You...you really...meant it?"

He looked at me in surprise for a moment, before he leaned in quickly and took my lips with his.

"You are my sultana. I shall have no other."

My heart quickened, and I thought I might faint.

"I hereby name Claudianne Jakard the rightful, chosen sultana of his majesty, Sultan Klaus Malik Jakard!" My father called out.

The man I didn't know repeated the sentence.

Qassim repeated the sentence.

The crowd began chanting "Sultan, Sultana! Sultan, Sultana!" ...and I thought that my heart would burst.

Klaus lifted me into his arms, and I sobbed into his embrace as he held me.

"Shh," he murmured into my ear. "I have you, Claudianne."

"But I...you..."

He met my eyes. "Please...just leave it to me, now. Trust in me. I promise, I will never hurt you. Can you do that?"

I felt my cheeks heat up...but I nodded.

Chapter 15 – Klaus Malik Jakard

I had Amir take Claudianne to the Sultan and Sultana's chambers, to get her healed by the physician and dressed in proper attire.

She had started blushing, looking over herself and the state that she was in...and I hadn't missed her condition.

She looked drastically thinner than she had been before. Her hair and body were dirty, covered in dirt and grime.

Her cheeks, once puffy and round, had sunken in a bit.

Her fingernails were just starting to grow back, and I could tell they had been ripped off.

The back of her gown had been covered in red lines, and I had quickly been informed that she had been whipped.

There was a thick, scarred brand on her right palm.

Oh, yes, I had many things to pay back to this sorry sack of shit before me on the ground, trembling as he glared up at me with hatred.

The moment I had been revealed under my true identity, he had started shaking, grunting and moaning at me through his gags with an enraged expression...because he knew what that meant.

If someone takes over the throne and there was already a legitimate heir, it meant that the one whom had taken the throne was deposed automatically.

It was because, since I was alive and healthy and there to take the throne as the legitimate heir, the only son of the last legitimate sultan-to-be, my claim was above Claudianne's claim to the throne.

Her ascendance to the throne was, therefore, disqualified and illegitimate, and void.

That meant that, by default, he was no longer sultan, either.

Everyone knew what that meant.

He had caused severe harm to members of the imperial family when he had wrongfully taken the throne, and had no claim to said throne. He had committed treason.

I looked to the new guards that Ciel had given me for my kingdom—because so many had joined the anti-mage faction, there had only been a handful left who were loyal to the royal family of my kingdom.

I pointed at Kasha. "Take this filth to the dungeons. Brand his right hand, rip off his fingernails, give him thirty lashes with the whip, and then leave him to starve in the dungeon for a month. If he is still alive, by that point? Tie him to a post at the gates of the kingdom, and let him feed the crows," I scoffed. "Congratulations, Lord Kasha. You are deposed and your marriage is void."

I turned, enjoying the screams through his gag, and the wonderful sound of him being slapped by the guards to silence him as I walked away.

I made my way into the palace with Ciel, the Archduke, Qassim, and a few others behind us.

We made our way into the throne room, and I sighed, plopping down on the throne.

"Well..." I sighed. "That...took longer than I had anticipated."

Ciel sighed, shaking his head. "There were a lot more anti-mage rebels than I expected," he said. "How did your country get into such a shape...?"

"I am not sure...but thank you, from the bottom of my heart, for helping us. Oh! Speaking of which..." I turned to Qassim. "Please ask Saffora to come here."

He nodded, shifting into his cat form and scampering off through the palace.

Ciel gaped after him. "Alright, that...has to be one of the coolest things that I've ever seen!" He said, giddy like a child.

"...How old are you?" I laughed.

He laughed, too. "Twenty-one. I told you; I haven't been the emperor for much time. And there is still much that I haven't seen in this world. Deserts and sand palaces, for one. The structure of this palace is totally different than mine; even the halls, the ornate beauty of the rooms...it is such a rich culture, despite how diverse and different it is from my own. I hadn't really known what to expect. My mother had tried to describe it to me, but nothing I had ever pictured even comes close."

I smiled. "I am glad you like it, then, Ciel."

He grinned. "I do, Klaus. So—"

We heard voices coming back, and we glanced to the side to see Saffora, following the cat form of Qassim.

"I have brought her," Qassim said, plopping down.

"He can even talk in that form?" Ciel laughed, before his eyes caught on Saffora. "Oh…wow," he breathed, eyes wide.

"…." She didn't say anything. Her eyes remained locked on the young emperor.

"Saffora Setz, allow me to introduce you to Ciel Twilight—the Emperor of the Western Empire."

She flinched, and immediately bent into curtsy. "Oh, my, I apologize," she said, soft. "It is my pleasure to make your acquaintance."

He smiled, and stepped down the steps toward her. "No," he smiled warmly. "It is mine."

He bowed at the waist, and all of us gaped at the open display of affection as he lifted her hand to his lips, kissing the back of her hand.

She blushed prettily, batting her lashes at him and smiling at him.

I thought, in that moment, that this would go very smoothly, then. She was very interested. He was certainly a handsome man, and very suave. He flashed his teeth in a grin, looking like a naughty little boy. The corners of his eyes crinkled; his eyes bright with mirth.

"Would you consider, my lady…becoming an empress…?"

Her eyes went wide, her face flushed, and she stumbled back a bit.

"M-m-me…? M-me, an em-empress…?" She asked, face flushed red. "I…I…Oh," she gasped…before she fainted.

I chuckled as he fluttered about like a butterfly, distressed and flustered over her reaction.

Some maids rushed over, wiping off her head with a cool wet cloth and fanning her with paper fans.

"You have your blushing bride," I grinned at Ciel.

"I-I was just trying to flirt! I wasn't trying to make her faint, honest."

I smiled. "Suuuure," I said, dragging out the word.

"If I had known she would faint, I would have made a more…delicate approach," he said, blushing as he fussed over her.

She started coming to, and looked around before her wide eyes settled on him.

"I am sorry, my lady, I hadn't meant to startle you. I was just flirting with you, but what I said…I meant it in earnest, honest! I would…like very much to get to know you, and for you to become my empress."

She blushed. "I…but I…I am just a noblewoman—"

"My mother is just a noblewoman from a dwindling noble house in this nation, too," he smiled. "My family has ancestors who married into this kingdom, too. Please…don't say that you are unfit or that you do not match me. You…are stunning. You remind me of the portraits of my mother at your age, and you carry the same air of decorum and grace. Please…consider me?"

She gaped at him, before she blushed and gave a nod. "If you are certain…then…I would like to get to know you, too."

He grinned. "Yes!" He smiled.

I smiled at them warmly. Everything seemed to be working out well.

I truly hoped for the best for my cousin, and for Saffora. She had always been a faithful handmaiden and friend to my bride.

We turned when the doors opened, and in walked the physician…with a somber look on his face.

I leapt up from the throne, rushing to him.

"What did you find?"

"Well," he said, clearing his throat. "She will heal fine," he said first. "But there are marks that make it evident that she…tried to take her own life, in the dungeons."

My blood seemed to turn to ice in my veins, and everyone in the room grew very quiet.

"She has some infection in her back, from not being tended to properly. Her brand is very heavily melted flesh—it was held on too long, and they dragged the rod off after her flesh had melted to it." He sighed. "Her fingernails are growing back just fine, thankfully, and she will be able to get back to a normal weight with small meals taken at regular intervals during the day. I am, however, worried about the Mane-Lock. It needs to be filtered out of her system, and we will require at least one high-leveled mage and her mage root source."

I grinned. "I am her mana root source…and Qassim can join me."

He gaped at me. "You are, sire?"

"Yes," I said, nodding. "Why?"

"No, it's just...usually, only soul mates are mana roots, if it isn't a parent."

...Soul mate...

"Even though we are relatives?"

He shook his head. "I've never seen it in relatives outside of direct child-parent roots or sibling roots."

"Oh," I breathed.

Then...was this really a special case...?

I turned, rushing out of the room, and Qassim followed me with the physician.

When we arrived to the Sultan and Sultana's chambers, she was lying in bed, unconscious.

I imagined that she hadn't gotten much rest in the last two months, and I smiled sadly at her as she breathed deeply.

Now, there was only three things that I wanted to set right for her:

Firstly, I wanted to give her a proper wedding, where she both looked and felt beautiful and at peace, totally a willing participant and happy to get married. I wanted her to be a happy bride, and a proper sultana.

Secondly, I wanted to give her ability to use and control mana back, and teach her how to implement it. I wanted to give her that freedom and power.

Lastly, I wanted to make love to her—not just have her, physically, but truly make love to her and give her a child...one that wouldn't be forcefully miscarried. One that could, possibly, make it to full term and be born safely, without taking that away from her.

Above it all, though, I wanted her to be happy. I wanted her to be at peace and happy with her life. I would do anything in my power to achieve that.

I wanted to do those things for her, and I wouldn't rest until I made it happen.

I sat on one side, and the physician had my father sit on her other side.

The emperor, Ciel, and the others, came to the room to sit and watch, waiting and praying with us.

"Qassim, take her right hand and gently make an incision in her right palm, then set her hand into this bucket here—but don't let go of her arm."

Qassim gave a solemn nod, and a deep breath...before he did it.

"Your majesty, make a small incision in your left hand, and her left hand—clasp them together."

I did so.

"Now...Qassim, pull with your mana—feel for the poisonous herbs in her system, and filter through them. Pull the toxin out. Your majesty, push with your mana—push your mana and some of your blood into her, willing it to chase out the toxin."

Dark, dark black liquid, like dirty oil, began to drip rapidly into the bucket.

Qassim and I began to sweat with the effort it was taking.

The toxin was hanging onto her very bones, fighting to stay in her body.

We could almost mentally picture it.

We continued to push the flush through for over three hours, waiting and getting weary...

When, shortly after the fourth hour...the last of the black fluid started to get thinner and lighter, and finally, all that came out was blood.

"You did it!" The physician said, grinning brightly. "You flushed out her system. Now, all she needs is to rest. She will need time to recover, so please have some patience...but the worst is over for now. How are you feeling?" He asked, throwing a glance at me.

I sighed. "Tired...but I feel even heavier than before."

He came over, checking my pulse, along with Qassim.

"Your mana has entirely solidified," they both confirmed, and Qassim hugged me.

"Congratulations, my son. You have found your mana root, and solidified your mana."

To think that just a few years ago, I hadn't even been able to access my mana...

It was all because of this beautiful, wonderful young woman...

My woman.

Chapter 16 – Claudianne

I groaned as I awoke, having the most restful sleep I'd had in years.

I could hardly believe how well-rested and nicely weighted that I felt.

I...wait a moment...

I didn't feel...*empty* anymore.

What happened?

Why did I feel so warm and peaceful?

Wait, was I alarmed by even that, now? Had it been so long since I had been warm and peaceful that I was alarmed when I felt that way?

That was depressing...

I sat up slowly, looking around.

A couple of faces that I recognized—Klaus's young male attendants—jumped up from their seats.

"Your majesty!"

"You're finally awake!"

I cringed at the loud voices, but I smiled. "...What happened...?"

"You were asleep for a few days, your majesty," one told me.

"His majesty and Lord Sorcerer Qassim spent hours filtering the mana-hindering herb, Mane-Lock, out of your system! His majesty confirmed that you are one another's mana root, so he was able to force it out and solidify both of your mana!"

Klaus...had done all of that...?

"Where...is his majesty now?" I asked.

They both smiled at me. "Waiting for you to wake up, your majesty. He is working on paperwork right now."

"He will be so happy to know you're awake!"

"Oh, and Lady Saffora is going to become an empress in the Western Empire!"

I gaped at them.

It seemed that, apparently, a lot of things had happened during my unconsciousness...

"Is she finally awake?" I heard a voice say, and my father stepped in with a look of stark relief...and wrinkles. Exhaustion. He was so worn down.

This who situation had drastically aged him, and I could see the years taken off of his life in his face.

Still, he looked happy to see me.

"Thank the heavens," he murmured, hugging me. "I...I am so, so sorry, Claudianne."

"...Sorry...?" I asked, hugging him back.

He pulled away from me, levelling me with a somber expression I wasn't used to seeing on his face.

"I...I knew that Klaus was the hidden prince. I only suspected it, at first, but when we noticed your reactions to one another, the mana reaction...and we saw Qassim, and how vague he was about things...I knew that something had happened. We had suspected that he was from your eldest uncle's line, because we hadn't known that the middle son had a child on the way."

"...Why?" I asked.

"We didn't say anything because—"

"No," I said, shaking my head. "I mean, why did nobody know that? Why did you think that he was the eldest son, Bilad Jakard's son? Why would nobody know that the middle son, Bilal Jakard—who was murdered before his ascension to the throne—had a son on the way?"

He looked away. "They hid the pregnancy well. Only a handful of people knew. The most trusted of maids and Qassim. Right as the second tragic night—the murder of Bilal Jakard and Aya Osman—started, they...they abandoned Klaus in the floor. Qassim is the one whom rescued the baby and took him into hiding."

I gaped at him, horrified. "...Abandoned?" I asked. "How...how could any mother or father do that?" I choked back tears.

He shook his head. "I do not know. I believe that they must have felt that if they fled the palace and left the next heir, the anti-mage rebels would just leave it at that. They were caught and executed, while Qassim managed to escape with Klaus."

Tears welled in my eyes. "The Abandoned Prince..." I whispered.

He nodded. "Yes. I never told you, nor said anything to anyone else, because I knew that his claim would be stronger than your own. You begged me, pled so violently not to make you marry Kasha…and I heard about your visions. I left that information locked down, so that in case things did go awry, Klaus would be able to step up and prove his legitimacy as the true heir, and set you free from being sultana, and void Kasha's status as the sultan.

I gazed at him in shock. "You mean…you knew I had a way out, and that's why you left it as-is…"

"Yes," he said, looking ashamed. "I didn't know if your visions would come to pass. I had hoped that Kasha would become a good husband; a good sultan. I didn't want to put Klaus in danger, either. I knew about Qassim's sister, having been married to the emperor of the Western Empire, and I knew that if anything happened to you, he could journey there and return with aid—or at least, I hoped that would be the case. Had I known that the two of you…held such affections for one another, sooner, I…"

"Father…"

"I would have wed you to him, if I had known, Claudianne. I would have sent him right away to get aid, after telling him the situation with the anti-mage faction, and I would have sent him to bring back an army to drive out the rebels. Then, I would have let him take your hand in marriage. You…you wouldn't have had to suffer this way. I never suspected that the two of you had intimate feelings like this, but when he named you as his sultana, I…I realized just how completely and utterly I have failed you. I am sorry, my child."

Tears ran down my cheeks, my heart thumping hard and a lump in my throat from the emotion clogging it, and I took him into a tight hug.

"Thank you, father."

"The two of you have my blessing," he said. "Not that either of you need it, really, but you have it nonetheless."

A couple of hours passed by, before Klaus returned to the chambers where I was staying.

He took my hand, and kissed it. "Welcome back home, my love," he told me. "Did you sleep well?"

I nodded. "Yes…"

"We still have much to plan," he grinned at me. "But I wanted to get busy with paperwork and management of things around here, where you had left off. You have done exceedingly well, no thanks to someone," he said, scoffing. "He never deserved you, nor this title. But now, you can be a true sultana—you can consult with me on the ruling of the kingdom, and we can do this. Together."

My heart grew so full, and my chest felt tight. My affection burned so brightly for this man before me, sitting on the edge of the bed and holding my hands so tenderly to his face, pressing light kisses against my fingers.

I had gone through so much…but if I could be with this man, live in peace for the remainder of my days…it might just be worth it all.

"So," he said. "Would you like to begin planning an official wedding ceremony?"

I looked at him in surprise. "I…thought we already—"

"You were named my sultana," he smiled. "But there was no official ceremony, nor a reception banquet, nor…a bedding," he said, wagging his brows at me, and I smacked at his arm playfully, laughing.

"I don't need one," I told him. "As long as I can be with you, I don't need a ceremony or anything else," I said, pulling him closer to me.

He trembled, pressing a kiss to my lips. "I want to give you everything that he ruined for you," he told me. "I want to make up his hatred to you with love, Claudianne."

"Klaus…" I whispered, and he leaned back into me, his lips pushing against mine and his tongue licking into my mouth.

He pulled away. "I want to make it official, ceremonial…all of it. I want to watch you walk toward me in a wedding gown, and take official vows with you. I want to carry you to our chambers—shared chambers—and undress you, slowly; reverently," he murmured into me ear. "I want to love you the way you always deserved…and I don't want to feel like it is forbidden. I want everyone in the palace to know that it is our wedding night, and that I am engraving you into my body."

I trembled slightly, overcome with emotion and shivers of anticipation.

"Will you marry me, officially?" He murmured, and I gave a nod.

"Yes," I whispered.

"Good," he said, smiling.

June, 142 IY

It was the first day of June, and I awoke to a room full of flowers. My favorite—Roses.

Red Roses.

My handmaiden, who was about to leave in order to become the empress of the Western Empire, insisted on fulfilling her final duty to me as my handmaiden—helping me to get ready for my wedding.

My true wedding, the only one that counted.

The only one that I had ever wanted.

She rushed me to the bath, helping me file my nails and paint them. She helped me scrub my feet, and apply special oils and lotions to myself after the bath.

She left my beautiful peppery hair down.

I stepped into a sheer wrap that covered my private areas and hips, and wrapped another sheer wrap around my chest.

She helped me dress in a stunning, traditional, modest, floor-length gown with red sashes wrapping around my torso.

Red rose patterns were embroidered into white gown.

Red roses were settled into my headpiece.

When I caught sight of myself in the mirror, I looked absolutely stunning.

She lined my eyes with red shadow, black mascara, and black liner. My lips were stained a beautiful, bright red, accentuating their thickness well.

She wiped her forehead, admiring her handiwork.

"You are ready, your majesty," she smiled at me. "Are you excited?"

"Yes," I smiled, tenderly.

So much had happened to get us here.

So much had happened in such a short amount of time.

I had only been newly thirteen, when I had married Kasha.

Now, it had been two years, and I was finally getting to live the life that I should have been able to be living for the last two years.

Klaus...

Klaus had made it happen.

I would never be able to repay him.

My father waited for me outside of my chambers, and beamed a smile at me when he saw me.

"Oh...you look lovely," he told me. "Radiant...and so much like your mother."

I smiled, and hugged him. "Thank you, father."

"Come. Let's get you married to the right sultan this time."

I smiled up at him. "Yes," I said.

We made our way through the corridors—which had thankfully been repaired and cleaned—and met many servants along the way, who all bowed and congratulated me.

This...this was what I had expected the first time.

This was tradition.

It was already much different than my first wedding.

We stepped into the throne room, where a priest and Qassim stood on the steps before the throne, and Klaus stood below them, on the floor.

He was radiant.

He wore red, with white and purple sashes over his chest—an official sultan's formal uniform.

He looked to me when his father and the priest noticed me, and his face melted into the warmest expression I had ever seen him make.

It made butterflies erupt in my belly, and I trembled, suddenly anticipating the rest of the evening.

My father chuckled at my side. "If only I had known," he murmured.

We closed the distance between Klaus and I, and my father placed my hand into Klaus's.

"I give you my blessing, and gift you my daughter's hand in matrimony. Do not hurt her," he said.

Klaus nodded his head, solemn. "I would sooner die."

My father was satisfied with that, and moved to take his seat, along with everyone else.

"We are gathered here to join these two in holy matrimony. Though not the first wedding for the sultana, perhaps this time, it will be the right one," he said, giving an affectionate expression. "Congratulations to you both. Sultan Klaus Malik Jakard—do you take the princess, Claudianne Jasmine Jakard, as your lawful bride and official Sultana?"

"I do," he proclaimed, loud and proud.

"Do you, Princess Claudianne Jasmine Jakard, take the Sultan, Klaus Malik Jakard, as your lawful husband and official Sultan?"

"I do," I smiled up at him.

His smile was victorious, his shoulders pulled back in pride.

He looked like he had just won the world's hardest competition. I supposed it was, to him.

"I pronounce you, proudly and with love, as Sultan and Sultana. You may kiss your bride," he said.

As Klaus leaned in to kiss me, lights like fireworks—without the booms—shined all over the throne room, and the crowd gasped and awed at the sight of it.

Klaus grinned like a happy little boy, taking my hand in his and tugging me with him out of the room.

We laughed as we made our way to the banquet hall, where we were joined by all of our family and friends as we enjoyed a hearty meal and desserts and fine wines.

Feelings I had never experienced filled me as Klaus announced that he was going to consummate his marriage, because nobody else knew that we'd already been intimate before, and rushed me through the halls to our newly renovated shared chambers that he'd been having worked on for the last two weeks.

He carried me to the bed, and sat me gently in a bed covered with red rose petals.

"Now, Claudianne…I shall take you as my rightful bride," he smiled.

He began with my hand—my right hand.

He pressed kisses all over the palm, moving slowly to each finger, the wrist, up the forearm and bicep to my shoulder.

He kissed and sucked on my neck and throat.

He kissed me deeply, licking his way around my mouth and I enjoyed the taste of wine on his tongue.

He moved to the other side of my neck and throat, my left shoulder, down my bicep and forearm and my left wrist, my left hand, my left palm.

He moved back to kiss me, before trailing a path of blazing fire down my throat with his tongue, and he sucked and nipped my collarbone.

He unwrapped my wedding gown, and found my hardened nipples through the sheer fabric of my under wrappings.

He chuckled. "Oh," he said. "You're enjoying this," he murmured as he nibbled one trough the fabric.

I moaned, and he used a little bit of teeth to gnaw on it softly before he began to flick the other.

"I shall please you to the utmost of my capabilities, my bride," he promised.

Chapter 17 – Klaus

The feeling of her hardened nipples against my tongue…it was bliss.

I swirled them each, round and round, enjoying her natural taste.

I could taste oils and a light lotion, but they were harmless.

They only added to her natural flavor; the taste of jasmine and rose infused tea.

I stroked her sides and torso, her ribcage, with my fingers, before I trailed my tongue along the same paths.

She gasped, thrusting her chest out, bowing toward me.

She was so responsive to me, that it made my dick harden so thick and full in my trousers.

I suddenly felt the need for freedom, but I restrained myself.

Tonight, was about Claudianne.

I could focus on what I wanted for myself at a later time, I was certain.

Her airy gasps and moans spurred me on, and I unwrapped the sheer fabric from around her hips and over her lower regions.

Then, bypassing that area, I moved to kissing and nipping down her inner and outer thighs. Her knees and calves, paying special attention to the erogenous zones I had carefully been storing in my memory from our first lovemaking session.

I had done my best to memorize her preferences, and I was not disappointed by the results as she cried out.

I glanced up at her—surprisingly shaved—pussy, and I felt myself harden like a rock when I saw the slick gleam of wetness coating her.

Her slit parted for a flap of skin that I knew was sensitive, a pretty little bud of a clit settled into that cushion at the top.

It was cliched, and of poor taste, but it still reminded me of a flower, somehow, with the skin acting as petals.

Everything about her, though, reminded me of a flower.

I held her to the highest, most precious regard.

Delicate, easily damaged, and to be handled with the utmost of care…or else she would wilt and wither away, as she had under Kasha's negligence and abuse.

I would help her to flourish.

Starting with our lovemaking…because even now…

Even now, she trembled softly, a frightened look on her face.

Years of trauma and forceful bedding had instilled her with fear, and I wanted to teach her that I could bring her pure love and pleasure…if only she would allow me to do so.

I sucked her toes, one by one, into my mouth, swirling them around, and she gave me the exact reaction I had hoped for—she squealed, and laughed as she tried to tug away from the ticklish sensation, whining that this was dirty and silly.

I just chuckled and kept on suckling, ignoring her.

I licked the arch of her foot, and she nearly came off the bed with a hard, sharp moan, before relaxing her body.

"Ohh," she cried. "Don't—don't stop, please," she begged.

Much to her dismay, however…I did.

I pulled myself up to rest my shoulders between her thighs, and parting the lips, I dove my tongue into her soaking pussy.

"Ah!" She sobbed, tears squeezing out of her eyes as she pulled. "K-Klaus!"

"Look how wet you are for me," I said softly, taking her hand and running it over her. "You know what's funny? Every time that I lick you," I said, giving her a good lave with my tongue for emphasis and feeling her walls clench down on my fingers. I tugged softly, showing her that she was squeezing me. "Your insides beg me to stay by squeezing my fingers."

"Ohh," she moaned unsteadily, wiggling her hips.

I chuckled as I dove back in, licking and sucking her lips and her clit thoroughly.

I turned my hand to face palm up, and curled my two fingers to hit a certain point inside of her on the front wall.

She cried out, slapping her hips up, and I sped my tongue rapidly over her clit.

It was only seconds before she seized, calling my name as she thrashed her hips up and down, begging for mercy.

"Good," I smiled up at her, crawling up her body. "I got you to cum for me. Now," I said. "I will enter your body, and we will become one."

She shivered, "Kl-Klaus…"

"Yes?"

I pushed in, gently pushing slowly until the entirety of my cock was inside of her hole.

"Klaus!" She called.

"Yes, Claudianne?" I chuckled, thrusting softly.

I would not beat it into her.

I wouldn't go fast; not this time, at least.

"Klaus!" She moaned as I slowly pulled back and entered her again at a languid pace.

"Yes, Claudianne?"

She sobbed, reaching up and clinging to me, bringing me down to kiss her.

My body curled over hers as I cradled her, kissing her and sucking her tongue.

I pulled back, sitting back on my knees and pulling her hips up to rest over mine. She still rested on her back, but her ass was lifted up, resting on my thighs.

I slid into her deeper than before, and I reached down and spread her lips wide, watching myself slide in and out of her.

"You are so beautiful," I told her.

She moaned sensually—a new moan that she hadn't made yet.

"Oh, yes," I said, stroking again, slowly. "Yes, make that moan again. I like the depth of the pleasure in it," I said.

I reached my thumb to her clit, and gave slow, sensual circles.

"Ahhh," she moaned. "Klaus," she pleaded. "Klaus, please…"

"Keep going," I said, my voice getting tight.

"K-Klaus, I want you…!" She said. "I want your seed inside of me. I want everything of you," she moaned.

"Ah, fuck," I murmured. "Moan for me, Claudianne," I said, moving a little faster inside of her, but my thumb still slow. She moaned again, a little louder and longer. "Yes, that's right, moan for me."

She moaned louder. "Klaus," she dragged out my name, pleading, her eyes squinted as her breasts bounced.

"Moan *louder*, my sultana!" I shouted, smiling victoriously as I felt the flutters of her orgasm approach. "I shall deliver the crowned prince into your womb, and you shall bear me a child with my seed!"

"Ah!" She sobbed, her walls shuttering around me as I was coated in her thick, sticky white cum with a hard rub over her clit, and she thrashed desperately as she orgasmed. "Yes! Yes, sultan, I shall bear you a son!" She sobbed. "Give your seed to my womb!"

"Fuck!" I shouted, slapping into her one last good, hard time, burying all the way into her as far as I could. "Fuck, yes, you pussy is so damn tight on my cock, Claudianne! My sultana!"

I felt her clenching and shuttering over me all over again, cumming over my cock once more, and she shrieked my name.

"Yes, sultan, yes! Klaus! Klaus!"

"Yes, my sultana," I laughed, leaning over her, and kissing her deeply. "Always call me with pleasure, and I will give you all I can give," I said. "Even until my very last breath in this life."

When she had fallen asleep with my cock still buried into her pelvis, I stroked her cheek and kissed her there before I let my softening manhood slide out of her body.

I strode over the basin, and got a warm wet cloth to wipe the excess mess from her before I covered her with the blankets, and I crawled beneath them with her.

I curled my body around her, spooning her, and she pushed her back further into the warmth of my chest, moaning softly.

I chuckled. "You are the beat of my heart, Claudianne. My very soulmate."

I fell into a restful, peaceful sleep.

The following morning came, and Claudianne spent her day resting in the newly renovated gardens, enjoying the peace and quiet.

I decided to spend the day with her in cat form—she adored my cat form.

She laughed and giggled as she stroked my luxurious and shiny coat, and smiled at me as she told me how happy she was.

Finally.

She took some time to spend with her friend, who had decided to, indeed, move to the Western Empire and become the empress.

I spent some time with Ciel while she did, and as we sat there and watched our women, he grinned at me.

"You finally look whole," he told me.

I smiled at him. "Thank you. If not for you…this wouldn't have been possible."

"We are family," he said. "And I must insist that you visit us soon, to show the sultana a world outside of this one."

I grinned at him. "I will uphold that."

"Good. I will extend an invitation."

The following day arrived quickly, and Claudianne cried when the ship pulled out of the port.

She turned to find me in my cat form, and laughed as she picked me up and stroked me.

"You know, I think seeing other kingdoms would benefit our kingdom," I told her.

I didn't tell her that I was already planning a trip...not yet.

August, 142 IY

Things had been running smoothly in the last two months, and Claudianne was an active participant in the rule of the city—at my side, not doing all of the work on her own.

We had interrogated Kasha's family, and found out that they were the ones whom had instigated the murders of all of the members of the imperial family. They, with their connections, had finally admitted to and been convicted of treason. We had peace, at last.

Their original goal, from the beginning, was to kill the sultans and sultanas until there was a singular female heir, and then, marry Kasha to her and have him drive out the remainder of the mage-blooded citizens.

Mage-hunts, plain and simple.

We had them convicted, and we were finally able to move forward on that front, thankfully.

We had even managed to find homes for Kasha's children. The eldest, the one whom had been named as the crowned prince, was given to Amir to raise as his own.

The others, to avoid being raised to hate the sultan and sultana, were given to other soldiers who were married and were willing to raise them as their own.

The concubines, who acted repentant only because Kasha had lost his status, were banished from the palace.

The harem was completely disbanded after a certain incident when, almost warily and cautiously, Claudianne had asked me if I intended to install my own harem.

I had looked at her in shock, which she misinterpreted as shock that she had even asked—a confirmation, in her mind.

I quickly took her into my arms, asking her how she could dare to ask me such a horrible, senseless question.

She was the only woman I wished to warm my bed and carry my seed.

She had tearfully cried and thanked me, pleading with me to forgive her for thinking so lowly of me…but when she had asked Kasha, he had been offended that she would ask and think he wouldn't say yes.

I decided, that night, that she needed to see some of the world, to help her heal and get her mind off of the sleaze-ball that was rotting, tied on a pole outside of the city gates with a sign that read, "This is what happens to traitors against the Sultan and Sultana."

Then, I got the excuse that I had been waiting for; a wedding invitation.

I quickly managed to find two trusted advisors—Qassim and one whom had stayed from the soldiers and mages that Ciel had brought—to help manage things, while Claudianne and I took a vacation.

Amir would be staying, overseeing Qassim's safety…just in case.

I put a blindfold on my wife, and led her through the city, silently shushing everyone and using a silencing spell until we reached the port so that she wouldn't know what was going on.

Behind us, my two boy attendants, who were quickly becoming strapping young men, carried our two bags.

We were travelling light there, because I didn't expect to be travelling light back.

We reached the ship, and I led her on board.

She stumbled and cried out when the boat rocked, and she froze, seemingly realizing what was going on.

"Are we…on the water?" She asked.

"We are," I told her, and I took off her blindfold.

She saw our guards, and my two attendants, as well as two maidservants for herself, and she gaped at me.

"Are…are we—?"

"Yes, my sultana," I said, loving the blush that always overtook her cheeks when I called her by that name. I smiled, pulling her into me and pressing my lips onto hers. "We are going to the Western Empire for a visit. We received the invitation yesterday—to Ciel and Saffora's wedding."

Tears filled her eyes, and she laughed and hugged me.

"Oh, Klaus! Thank you!"

I hugged her, and we looked out over the railing of the ship as the engine roared to life.

Chapter 18 – Claudianne & Klaus

September, 142 Imperial Year

Unfortunately…the seas were not kind to my body.

I had spent almost the entire trip sick, but thankfully, there had been a handful of good moments.

Moments where Klaus held my hand as we sat on the bow together, where he kissed me deeply every time we saw the sunset together.

When we reached the Western Empire, I nearly threw myself to the ground in reverence of solid land.

"Thank you for land!" I cried up to the heavens, and Klaus burst out laughing at me.

"Good heavens," he chuckled. "You would think you were going to die on that ship."

"I was starting to suspect that I might!" I cried, playfully smacking his arms.

He chuckled. "Yes, I know, love. You just…got seasick, badly. Let's get up to the palace and get settled and rest, yes? We can sightsee before the wedding in two days. We made it just in time."

She beamed up at me, before rapidly taking in her surroundings.

Klaus

This time, the party to welcome us was even grander than the one that had welcomed me when I had come by myself—probably because I had told Ciel and we were both certainly coming, and that she was getting the trip as a surprise.

He'd pulled out all the stops, having the knights pull out their swords and lift them up high, holding them up like a tunnel for us to pass through.

Claudianne giggled and smiled, enjoying the strange custom—before she rushed to the side of the dock, just over the water, and began to vomit.

They all gaped at her, shocked and concerned expressions on their faces.

"She has had severe seasickness," I informed them. "We are very thankful to be back on dry land."

They all turned sympathetic, nodding in understanding.

They should, considering that most of them, who had been on the journey with us to the Jakard Imperial Kingdom, had also faced seasickness during the trip.

It was a miracle that we had managed to defeat Kasha's army so soundly, considering how sick the soldiers and mages had been during the month-long journey to our homeland.

Some of our guards enjoyed reuniting with former coworkers, laughing and smiling and talking about the last couple of months as we made our way up to the palace…but I worried for Claudianne.

She had become quite pale, and looked somewhat green.

I hoped that her seasickness would wear off, quickly.

We reached the palace, finally, and made our way in to the throne room, where Ciel was waiting for us.

"Sultan! Sultana! How wonderful it is to see you both, Klaus and Claudianne, my dear cousins!" He said, standing and rushing to hug us both…until he noticed Claudianne's state. "Oh, dear," he said, sympathetic. "Seasickness?" He asked.

"I hate to report that she suffered with it in severity on the ship," I said.

"Oh, no," he said. "We have some medicine, here, to help with that nausea. Would you like to see if that helps?"

She nodded weakly, and he sent a maid to fetch the doctor.

"Thank you, Emperor Ciel," I smiled at him.

We turned our attention to Saffora as she called to us from the door that led into the corridors for the royal family only, and rushed to us.

"Your majesties!" She beamed, excited. "It is so wonderful to see you both! You look—" she noticed Claudianne. "Seasickness?"

I nodded.

"We're getting the doctor to send some medicine," Ciel said.

"Oh, that medicine worked wonders for me!" Saffora chirped, cheering up. "I hope that will settle your stomach," she smiled.

Claudianne weakly looked around, trying to enjoy the view before hanging her head again, face green and moaning.

"Where are they?" Saffora whispered, looking around when Claudianne looked on the verge of vomiting again.

"Here!" The servant called, rushing in.

"Here we are! Thank you, Mira," Ciel said, taking it and handing it to Claudianne. "And here is some water. This is a pill, Sultana. You put the tablet on your tongue, and swallow it down with a sip of water. It will work the same way that your powdered medicines work in the Jakard Imperial Kingdom, but this is faster acting and stronger, since more medicine is condensed into it."

I looked at it in awe. "Oh, how does this work?" I asked, immediately interested in seeing the effectiveness and trying it out in the homeland.

She took the medicine, and we waited for a few moments while the emperor detailed the medicine to me, telling me about his team of doctors and scientists that had been cultivating this new form of medication.

Claudianne's stomach seemed to settle, and she requested to eat some apples and retire for the evening.

...*Apples.*

...Apples...?

Why did that ring a bell to me?

She followed Saffora through the palace to go to our chambers, and I glanced to Ciel.

"...Is she pregnant...?"

I shook my head. "She had...well, I know that had her cycle in July. I don't know about August, honestly. She was so sick with the seasickness...most of us were."

He considered that. "If she continues getting sick, we will bring her the best physicians in the country to check and see what is going on. Keep an eye on her. For now," he grinned. "How would you like to go out and see the Empire from my favorite spot?"

Claudianne

"Your majesty, are you feeling alright, now?" Saffora asked.

I nodded. "I seem to feel a little better for now."

She smiled at me. "I still cannot believe that I'm getting married, your majesty! I am so happy! His family is so nice, and it is so nice to have people here who understand my dialect despite my accent. I had been worried, but he had assured me that his mother was from our homeland, too, and so, most of the palace was very used to the dialect of the Imperial Language that came from our people."

I smiled at her. "I am thankful, Saffora. I am so happy for you. You deserve to be happy...after everything that you suffered through with me."

"Oh," she said, tearing up and hugging me. "I am sorry that I was not a better friend to you in your darkest times. When you gave up, I shouldn't have caved. I should have kept encouraging you. Had it not been for my parents telling me how silly it was to stick it out and hold on with you, I think I would have remained stronger."

"Your...your parents spoke against our friendship?" I asked.

She nodded. "Yes…" She sighed. "But I came back, because that was what felt right. You were my dearest friend…and when I thought about how much you must have been struggling to give up…I knew that I couldn't just abandon you. I came back."

I smiled, and hugged her again. "Thank you…my dear Saffora."

The rest of the day passed alright, and I felt somewhat okay…but I still felt unsettled. We went to bed without any issues, but the time zone was different than it was back home, and it felt…strange. As if my body wasn't supposed to be asleep at this time.

I tossed onto my side, away from Klaus as he slept, my mind tossed into a dream.

My dream was…*emotional*, to say the least.

I was sitting in the gardens, holding a newborn, with a toddler at my side.

It was odd, the toddler was transparent…I could see him in this dream, but I could see through him, as well.

My dream-self did not seem to notice him, however.

He beamed a smile at me, laughing as he danced around me, and pressed kisses to my cheek before pressing kisses to the baby's cheeks. I did not react, but the infant did.

The baby was wrapped in a blue muslin material, and his white hair was a stark contrast against his dark skin.

He stirred in my arms, whimpering and scrunching his face while the toddler jerked his hands over his open mouth, looking on in surprise and trepidation of having awakened the baby.

When the baby settled back into my arms with a peaceful exhale, the toddler released an exhale, too.

We sudden looked up to see Klaus approach us, dressed richly and fine, radiant and powerful. He grinned and us, and came to press a kiss to my lips.

He, strangely, did not look at the toddler…as if he couldn't see the boy. I wasn't able to see him, either, apparently.

Still, I knew he was there.

"How is the crowned prince, today?" Klaus asked, stroking a finger over the baby's forehead.

I chuckled. "Kaleem is well," I smiled up at him, and he kissed me again even as the baby—Kaleem—stirred again, moaning and whimpering.

Klaus grinned broadly as he scooped the baby delicately into his arms, pressing kisses to the baby's forehead and whispering blessings into his hair before he smiled at me.

"I love you, my sultana. You are my moon, and now, you have given me the brightest star in my sky, as well. My son."

I smiled peacefully at him, "And you are the sun, that ran away the darkness that was drowning me."

He came and kneeled down to my level, kissing me and licking into my mouth with a deep, sensual kiss.

"I am ready to put another baby into your womb," he said huskily. "I wish to gift you more seed."

I chuckled into his lips as he continued kissing me.

I jerked awake, feeling hot and wet…and I reached over to my husband.

I curled closer to him, my heart pounding as I suddenly felt the need to have him buried within me.

I undid the wrappings of his underwear, and let his cock out into the open beneath the blanket as I stroked him, stimulating him and pressing kisses and loving licks to the organ.

It slowly became harder and harder, and I began to suck on it, bobbing my head over it fast to get it fully prepared.

I reached between my legs with one hand, rapidly stroking my clit in frenzied circles, desperate to get myself close to ready to cum.

I felt his body stirring, and I could hear his groggy night-voice, thick and rough with sleep.

"C-Claud…?" He asked, and I could feel his torso tense as he sat up a bit. He groggily realized what I was doing, and I quickly had his attention. "Claudianne…" He murmured. "Oh, my *sultana*," he moaned, the thickness of his voice making me wetter.

I wiggled my ass a bit, moaning over his length.

His hands came beneath the blankets, pulling me gently upward, and he pulled me out from beneath the blankets and brought me up to him to kiss him deeply.

"What brought this on, love?" He chuckled sleepily.

"I had a dream," I said.

"Oh…? Did I make love to you in that dream?"

I giggled. "We were just starting. I woke up, wet and ready to have you buried inside of me, Sultan."

He "Hmm"'ed, and took my jaw in his hands as he gently turned my head, kissing me even more deeply, sucking on my lips and nipping them before his tongue swirled around with mine.

I gasped as his tongue swirled into the clavicle of my collarbone, and he nipped my breast through my silk robe.

"I don't have any patience tonight, Claudianne…you woke me to your mouth on my cock, so my body is already prepared to enter you…" he reached his fingers down into my core, and he chuckled. "Though, you feel quite thoroughly prepared all on your own." He met my eyes. "You are soaking wet, love."

He parted my legs, and immediately, his length sank into my body with a squelch, and he thrusted into me.

I gasped and moaned, enjoying the sounds of thwaps and shlops as our bodies messily met one another in a vulgar sounding symphony of erotic sex.

He turned me on my side, straddling my bottom leg and pulling my top leg to rest with my calf up on his shoulder as he curled over me and strove his cock into my pussy again and again.

He reached down, his thumb stroking over my clit in desperate quick, light circles, and it was no time until I fell apart.

"Yes, yes, fuck…moan for me, my sultana!" He groaned, before he slapped against my body a few more times. "I will give you my essence now," he grunted, before he let out a guttural groan and his cock throbbed thickly inside of me.

I felt his heat spurt up inside of me, and I trembled.

"Yes…give me all of you," I whispered.

"I will give you all of me that you can take inside of you, my wife."

I smiled up at him, and he gently pulled out of me before he got on his back, pulling me to curl into his side and rest my head on his arm and leaning in to kiss my forehead.

"I love you, Klaus."

"I love you, Claudianne."

Chapter 19 – Klaus

The wedding day arrived quickly, and Claudianne continued to be a bit groggy and sluggish…though, the nights were…

Blissfully orgasmic.

Each night we'd been here, she had woken me with my cock between those pretty thick lips of hers, with that devilish tongue swirling around my cockhead and driving me into oblivion.

I pulled on my uniform, glancing over at Claudianne as she sat back while the maids helped her get ready in a traditional gown from our homeland—a gift from my adopted aunt that she'd brought with her.

It turned out that they had similar builds, actually.

We were finally ready, and we entered the ceremony space. Ciel already stood there, donned in a uniform, and was waiting.

Music started playing, and the guards raised their swords like a tunnel.

A drumroll sounded, and Saffora stepped forward, led my Ciel's father, the former emperor.

He led her to Ciel, who took her hand, and as they recited their vows, I glanced at my bride.

Her eyes were bright with tears and she was sniffling, a big smile on her face...but her face was a bit pale.

I could see that she was struggling, but she was too distracted to be brought down by it in that moment.

They announced the couple as being husband and wife, and they kissed.

Everyone cheered, and we were all ushered to a banquet hall, where we were served all kinds of delicacies I'd only seen in this kingdom, as well as special options from our homeland that had been made to perfection.

Ciel's father and mother each took a turn making a speech, and I noticed Claudianne was looking a bit green again.

...Was she still feeling that sick...?

"And now, I would like to ask the Sultana of the Jakard Imperial Kingdom to say a few words to bless the happy couple," Ciel's mother said, smiling warmly. "Saffora served as a special, long-time childhood friend to the Sultana, and they were very close."

Everyone cheered, and I stroked a finger over my wife's hand as she stood. She glanced at me.

"Can you do this?" I asked in a whisper.

She gave a warm smile and a nod, and turned, heading up to the front and stepping onto the small stage that had been set up for this occasion.

"Saffora is my best friend," she smiled. "She has been my friend for as long as I can remember, and was always faithful at my side. She is a special..." She started to turn greener, and I perked up. "A very special...dear friend...who is like a sister to me..."

She began to sway, and I was up and out of my seat.

Ciel and Saffora were close behind me, calling for the physician.

Suddenly, just as we were getting closer to her, my wife began to vomit, falling to her knees and tears rolling down her face as she heaved.

Servants were quickly on the scene, a bucket beneath her face as others rushed to get a wet cloth against her forehead and another pulled her hair back to keep it out of the way.

"Get everyone adjourned outside for the fireworks," Ciel announced, directing everyone to go outside to the courtyard, where many chairs and tables were set up with desserts and wines to sit and watch the scheduled fireworks.

The physician rushed in quickly, and came to our side.

As Claudianne finished vomiting, and the servants helped to lift her and bring her something to change into, as well as a changing screen to help her out of her soiled clothes, she sobbed and covered her face with her hands.

"I'm so sorry," she moaned. "I…I'm sorry, I ruined your banquet!"

"No!" Ciel rushed, patting her on the back. "No, no, Claudianne. You didn't ruin it. You just…pushed the events forward a little, that's all. Nothing is ruined," he said, soothing comfort in his tone.

"That's right, your majesty. Your health is more important than a banquet."

The servants set up the changing screen, and I helped her get wiped up and cleaned and changed into fresh clothes.

Then, the physician who had been waiting patiently came to her side as we sat her down.

His hands glowed as they hovered over her chest and belly, and then he checked her pulse and asked her a few questions.

"Have you felt nauseated for long?"

"Since we got on the boat...but it hasn't stopped."

"...Not even after the medicine we gave?" He asked, surprised.

I shook my head. "No. She's also been tossing a lot at night, and waking up very..." I cleared my throat. "Very thoroughly interested in me," I said, coughing.

"Oh," the doctor said, eyes wide. He looked to her. "Any vivid dreams? Odd cravings? Wanting to eat more or less than usual around the nausea?"

She thought about this. "Yes, very vivid emotional dreams. No odd cravings, but I have been wanting to eat a little less because I'm scared of getting sick."

"You have been having cravings," Saffora chimed in. "You've wanted almost nothing but apples since you arrived."

I suddenly knew, as it hit me like a ton of rock, what was happening.

I didn't know how I hadn't realized it sooner, and now I knew why the apples had rung such a strong bell with me before, just days prior;

When Claudianne had gotten pregnant before, she had wanted almost nothing but apples then, too.

My heart began to pound, and I watched on in stupor.

"Sensitive to smells?"

"…A little," she admitted.

He grinned at her. "When was the last time you had your cycle?"

She calculated.

"I…I…I don't…?"

"June," I said. "Your last cycle was at the beginning of June." I shook my head. "I hadn't thought about it for July, because there was so much work and everything was going on around the kingdom. We were so caught up in things. And then, when we left in August, we were on the ship for the entire month, and most of us had seasickness. I wasn't even paying attention to your cycle, or lack thereof…but now that I think about it, you never bled during our time on the ship, either."

"And I've already…skipped this months' cycle," she said, gaping at me. "You mean…?"

I grinned at her. "Your last cycle was at the beginning of June. That means you could have conceived any time after then."

Ciel, who was grinning from ear to ear, looked to the doctor. "Is it safe to say she is, indeed, with child?"

The doctor nodded. "Certainly." He looked to me. "We actually…have technology, that can tell us how far along she is, what gender child you are having…we have made so many advancements, that you would be stunned."

I gaped at him before I looked to her. "Would you like to find out?"

She nodded, smiling softly as she cupped her belly. "Yes."

I helped her stand, and we were led through the halls as Ciel and Saffora went on out to the party, wishing us luck and telling us they would join us later.

We went to a lab, where there were machines and monitors and boxes with odd screens that were lit up, almost by magic.

What was this place?

"Everything is run by mana," a sorcerer grinned at us, stepping up to us. "The doctor just briefed me on the situation," he smiled. "You are expecting, yes? You want to know how far the gestation is, and the gender?"

"Yes, if you are able?" I asked.

He beamed at me. "Of course," he smiled. "This way." He directed Claudianne to lie back on the lounging chair, and pulled the gown up as he looked away, covering her privates and legs with a blanket. "Please pardon me, but I must have access to the torso, bare skinned." He took out a tube, and poured out some blue gel onto her skin before taking a strange object attached to a wire that led into the box with the lit-up screen.

An image came to life on the screen, and we were both transfixed as we saw a small, human-looking body moving minutely.

"That," the sorcerer grinned at us. "That is your baby, inside of the womb. Judging by the size and development here, it looks as if you are…just about to enter the second trimester already," he chuckled. "Around fourteen weeks or so, and the gender," he said, and he moved the object over her abdomen. Then, the image changed, and we could see what looked like two legs and a bottom. "Ah, yes, there it is," he said, pointing to a shape between the legs. "There is the penis. You are having a boy," he beamed at us.

"...The Crowned Prince," I deemed him.

"Kaleem," Claudianne whispered.

I looked to her. "Kaleem?" I asked.

She nodded. "I...I had a dream, Klaus. A dream of my angel at my side, looking over you and I and our baby...and we called the baby Kaleem."

I felt my heart pump thickly, and my chest was heavy as I was awash with emotion. "Kaleem," I repeated. We looked up to the sorcerer. "I want to bring this technology to my kingdom, and bring us into the new century. But for now, I want to return to the party, if we can."

"Thankfully, we have medicine to help with morning sickness," he told me as the doctor approached us. "The medicine we gave you before was specifically for seasickness, which explains why it only helped a little. This new medicine will help you to not get sick as much, but it is not a fix-all. We recommend apples and peppermint, and have a list of other good foods and other things to help," he said.

"Thank you," I said, pulling into a hug, and he looked surprised before he chuckled and returned the gesture. Then, I turned to my bride, and kissed her forehead. "Thank you, my sultana."

Then, we made our way back out to the party, and Ciel and Saffora caught sight of us and rushed over.

"Are you alright?" Saffora asked.

Claudianne nodded. "Yes," she smiled at them. "We have some news." She looked to me, and I smiled.

"We are, indeed, expecting a child. Claudianne is around fourteen weeks pregnant, and the child…we are having a son. The Crowned Prince…Kaleem."

"Oh," Saffora gasped, clasping her hands together over her mouth, eyes filling with tears. "Claudianne!" She cried, hugging her, even as Ciel pulled me into an embrace.

"Congratulations, Klaus," he smiled. Then, he turned to the crowd. "Attention! Attention, everyone!" He called, and everyone turned to face us. "Congratulations are in order! The Sultan and The Sultana of the Jakard Imperial Kingdom are expecting their first child together—a prince, the Crowned Prince to be, Kaleem!"

The crowd roared to life in cheer and congratulations, and we were embraced and received well-wishes.

We were able to enjoy some amazingly delicious dessert, before watching the fireworks from the safety of our bedchambers while Claudianne soaked in a warm bath and I massaged her feet, sucking on her toes and eyeing her with a thirst I'd never yet felt for her.

That night, I caressed her and lavished her belly and licked blazing paths over her before I sank my tongue between her pussy lips, sucking and tonguing her into oblivion.

I sank into her with such tenderness, cradling her belly and kissing her deeply.

As she came over me, trembling as I held her, my eyes burned with tears of affection and joy.

"Thank you, Claudianne. Thank you, my sultana. You bear the Crowned Prince, our son, in your womb, and I honor and bless you," I told her. Her eyes filled with tears, and she held me as she tearfully kissed me, thanking me.

We fell asleep wrapped up in one another, my cock still inside of her, and my hands wrapped around her even as she cradled her belly.

Tears ran down her cheeks as she snoozed, and I knew what was on her mind, in her dreams.

Her miscarried son.

She had been so attached, so determined to love him in spite of everything. She had been so ready to adore and spoil him and raise him as her star.

She deserved that child.

Despite how he had been conceived, she had loved and cherished him.

I knew that this pregnancy was a beautiful but bitter medicine for her.

She needed the baby to heal, and I wanted to give her children because I knew that she wanted children. She had told me that before...but...

I knew that it made her think about the child that she had lost...my step-son.

It made me want to have Kasha tortured and executed all over again.

Still, I couldn't help but to be overjoyed and excited at the news that I was a father.

It still didn't feel real.

October, 142 IY

"It is not advisable to take another month-long journey across the sea right now," the head sorcerer admitted. "However, as the Sultan and Sultana, I do understand that you cannot continue to remain in a foreign land. So, I have prepared some things for you, as a gesture of goodwill and by the instruction of the emperor and empress," he smiled.

"I have prepared medicines to last for the entire journey—medicine for you and your entire crew to fight seasickness, and medicine for morning sickness. I have also prepared an abundance of long-lasting, bland foods to help you not feel so nauseated."

"We have also prepared some machines and two sorcerers to go with you to show you how the technology works, train some workers, and show you the process of making pills. Together, we will help your kingdom advance, as you requested," the head sorcerer, Visage, told us.

I took his pale hand, and glanced up as his silvery hair and his light green eyes.

"Thank you," I said, and I smiled at him. "It has truly been a pleasure to get to know you all. Please, if you ever wish to come to our kingdom, send one of the homing-hawks with a request. We will give you a warm welcome," I grinned.

We turned to Ciel and Saffora, who hugged us and smiled at us.

"I will try to make the journey to see the new crowned prince when he has been born, but that will depend on circumstances," Saffora giggled to Claudianne. "Our efforts to have our own child have been…quite spirited," she laughed.

Ciel blushed, but grinned and winked at us.

"We wish you luck in the venture," Claudianne said. "I do hope that you will visit us, soon," she told them.

"Farewell, dear cousins. We will set up a time to visit soon, and we hope to greet a shining new star upon our arrival there," Ciel said.

With one last hug, we made our way to the docks, loaded up onto the ship, and began our trip home.

November, 142 IY

"You have done well in our absence," I grinned at Qassim in his cat form...who was grinning very broadly at me, even as a cat. "...What?"

"Oh, nothing, I've just...already heard the whispers from servants," he grinned. "She's pregnant?"

I laughed. "Yes, very obviously, now. She conceived in June, if you must know."

"Oh, wow," he said, turning into his human form and gaping at me. "So, she was already pregnant when you left, and pregnant when you journeyed back?"

"The trip there was horrible, with the seasickness and morning sickness. But the trip back was quite pleasant, actually. I have brought many new things for us," I said, motioning him to follow me, and I led him out of the office and into the reception hall, where Claudianne still sat, directing maids and butlers and monitoring everything. She noticed us and perked up.

"Qassim!" She grinned at him, and he bent to hug her in her seat.

"I heard the news, and I see it, too! I am so overjoyed for you, Sultana."

She beamed at him, even as Amir kneeled at her side and pressed a kiss to her knuckles in honor of her.

Other servants flittered over her, while Qassim and I turned our attention to the mages who had returned with me, and we began deciding where to construct a lab like the one that they had in the Western Empire.

We began working diligently, under their instruction, and within a few weeks, we were getting the hang of things.

It turned out that they were well-versed in being physicians, and they helped us to open a medical center and train doctors.

Many of the soldiers who had come here with me at the beginning of the year to take back the kingdom had met good women, settled down, and were expecting mage-blooded children of their own, as well.

Our small kingdom was growing, and we would soon be thriving.

February, 143 IY

It was the last day of the month, just a week before the due date, when Claudianne went into labor during her massage.

Thankfully, it was a mercifully quick labor, and she was only laboring for thirty minutes before she began to push.

Pushing only lasted about five minutes, and the baby arrived—healthy and whole and beautiful.

With his stunning dark skin, and his stark-contrast silvery-white hair.

He had his mother's thick pouty lips, and my nose.

He had high cheekbones and thick, beautiful eyelashes that framed bright, deep purple eyes.

He was absolutely stunning.

"Kaleem," I murmured, pressing a reverent kiss to his forehead and blessing him, letting my mana wash over his body to familiarize himself and his mana with my own.

This was a tradition for parents, in order to become a child's mana root.

I didn't want to take any chances. He may not meet a soul mate soon enough, and if that were the case, I wanted for him to have his roots solidified.

He squirmed a bit, his mana stirring with mine, and I chuckled.

"Yes, you are powerful, my son. Our little crowned prince."

"Thank you," I heard my wife whimper, and I glanced at her, bringing the baby to her face to see him.

"Thank you," I told her. "Thank you, my sultana. You have given me a son."

Epilogue – Claudianne

January, 145 Imperial Year

"Come on, my little love!" I cheered, watching Kaleem totter over to me. He held a stuffed lion doll in his fist, and laughed as he rushed me.

I scooped him up, and he squealed as I blew raspberries into his neck and tussled his hair.

I gasped as the child in my womb—another prince—kicked hard, and I laughed as I set Kaleem down onto his feet and rubbed a hand over my belly.

"Calm yourself, Cavell," I shushed him. "I am just playing with your brother."

Motherhood had been good to me.

Kaleem was a mild, sweet, even-tempered child, who had made very little fuss even as a baby.

He was gentle and affectionate, and truly gave me the greatest joy...but his favorite part of the day was when his father returned from his duties around the palace, and he got to play with him for the evening.

Klaus had been a very good father. He was warm and tender with our son, but also firm and fair. He made sure that Kaleem was being respectful toward me, and doing his part to learn and help.

Kaleem helped me with simple things, like cleaning up after ourselves and taking care of the plants.

He was a very good boy.

He was smart, too, learning his alphabet and numbers, colors, shapes, and so on.

We were a happy family, and I was finally at peace with my life.

"He's growing so fast," Ciel said, grinning at me as he held his seven-month-old in his arms. A son.

Saffora was one month behind me in her second pregnancy with a girl, and we'd already decided to raise our children as best friends.

Even if they were a world apart, they would be best friends. Possibly even lovers, one day, but that was up to them.

We watched Amir's sons, Aman and Assan, run and play with Kaleem. They were only a couple of years apart.

Amir's child on the way, a daughter, was already set to grow up with Kaleem as his future bride…because I didn't have anyone else as close to me in this kingdom as his family.

He was powerful, and loyal. His family had served the royal family for a long time.

His daughter was an excellent candidate.

The future seemed set, and we were ready for it.

Bonus Chapter 1 – Kaleem Jakard

March, 159 Imperial Year

"And do you, Asra Ali, take Kaleem Jakard to be your wedded wife and future sultan? Do you promise to be his honored sultana?"

"I do," she smiled tearfully up at me.

Her radiant smile, her silky, raven-black hair, and her golden eyes did me in.

I was sixteen, now, and had recently reached the newly legalized age of marriageability.

It had once been the age of thirteen, but mother had insisted that this age be increased by a few years, and father had agreed easily.

He was easily won over by my mother.

I'd had a very bright, loving childhood. I had a lot of family—grandfathers who loved me, many precious people who worked for us who looked out for me.

I had learned how to fight from Amir and his sons, and how to use my mana from grandfather Qassim and my father.

I was even learning the healing arts from the physician mages in the medical facility.

I was honoring my role as the crowned prince, and learning all that I needed to learn in order to lead our growing kingdom forward.

Now, I had just taken my wife—the daughter of Amir Ali, my mother's most trusted guard. He had been a bit older when she had been born, and so, he was in his early fifties, now, and had passed his role as guard over the sultana and princess to his sons.

There were several royal children.

There was the eldest prince, whom had been miscarried and never was able to take his first breaths in this world.

There was myself, the second eldest—the eldest living, the crowned prince. I was sixteen.

There was the second prince, Cavell, with his peppery grey and silver hair and light lavender eyes. He favored mother a bit more than I did. He was thirteen.

There had been a first princess, Kaia, who had passed away due to fever in the night when she was only one year old, and mother had been crushed for a couple of years. Kaia had been born when I was six.

Then, mother had finally had her last child two years later, when I was eight.

That child was the second princess, Kadi, with her bright silver-white hair and her dark purple eyes that were even more dark than father's. She was now seven, going on eight.

I was instructed to kiss my bride, and I did.

We made our way to the banquet hall, and ate a hearty feast before retiring to our chambers.

I decided that I was not ready to bed her just yet. I wanted more time to just spend with her naturally, without jumping straight into the bed with her.

She was happy about that, as she had been quite nervous, and we lie together, just spending the night talking and getting closer.

We kissed a few times, but we wouldn't make love for a while.

I was happy.

I was enjoying my life.

Bonus Chapter 2 – Cavell Jakard Luther

January, 160 Imperial Year

"Don't worry, mother," I laughed, hugging her. "I'll be alright. I am being adopted into one of the most prestigious noble families in the empire, and I will be courting the princess right away. We will be marrying within the year, I am sure."

She fretted over me, worrying and hugging on me even as my baby sister clung to me.

My older brother stood nearby, hugging his bride with his hand resting gently over her rounding belly.

They weren't far along in the pregnancy, yet. They had found out they were expecting twins, so the crowned princess was a bit larger than anticipated.

"I'll send letters, and I'll visit occasionally."

Mother's eyes welled with tears, and she hugged me to her. "Please, write me as soon as you arrive?"

"I will," I promised.

With final kisses and well-wishes, I set foot onto the ship and began my journey for the Western Empire.

Emperor Ciel and Empress Saffora's eldest daughter, Marielle—their second child who was just a few months younger than I was—was set to be my bride.

I was fourteen, now, so she was thirteen and a half.

It had been a pact of friendship and goodwill made by our mothers before we were born to have us marry when we reached the marrying age. I had met her a couple of times, but it hadn't been very often.

I knew what she looked like, thanks to a recent portrait made and sent with a letter designating that she had reached their legal marrying age and was ready for a husband.

There was just one issue—she had demanded to remain in her homeland.

She did not wish to travel to the Jakard Imperial Kingdom, because the sand and heat fatigued her and caused severe allergen reactions.

So, I was making my way to be adopted into the highest ranked noble family in their nation—who, surprisingly, had no son or legal heir.

I would be inheriting the title of Archduke, and the fief and wealth that came with it.

She would get to remain in the Western Empire, and I was gaining a wife and renown along with a title and land.

Mother may have been quite nervous about the ordeal, but the emperor and empress insisted that this family was loyal, kind, and happy to accept me.

March, 160 IY

She sighed as I sat and had tea with her, glancing off to the side.

"Is something wrong, princess?" I asked.

She sighed. "I just…didn't really want to get married. I haven't gotten to explore or even find myself. I don't want to give myself—someone I don't even know completely—over to someone else this way. It is too rushed."

I grinned at her. "I feel the same way," I told her. "After all, I was just adopted. I just became a 'Luther' and I'm still learning all about what that means. But I have a proposition for you." I smiled at her. "Our engagement will end in marriage by the end of the month, right? How about we spend our years until we ascend the title of duke and duchess travelling and getting to know one another, and finding ourselves?"

She gaped at me; eyes bright and filled with wonder. "Really?" She asked.

I smiled, taking her hands in mine. "Yes."

July, 161 IY

My bride, Marielle and I, were now a year older.

I was about to be sixteen, and she had recently turned fifteen.

We had spent the last year travelling, as we had promised.

We arrived to our destination, now, and smiled at the man who met us there.

"Welcome to the Northern Kingdom of Nias," the head sorcerer of the Northern Mage Tower greeted us. "We received the letter that you two would be travelling this way. I hope your trip has been pleasant?"

"It has!" My young bride gushed, lighting up. "We saw so many amazing sights, and beautiful scenery! We got to make some stops along the way, too. It was really fun."

He smiled. "I am glad to hear that you had a good journey. I have a room prepared for you both, and dinner happens in an hour. Please pull on the rope in your room whenever you require assistance," he said.

We reached our chambers, high-up in the tower, with an amazing view of that overlooked the sea and mountain range in the distance.

There was a single bed, and we both looked at one another and blushed.

We hadn't yet consummated our marriage. We had been married for over a year, now, but we were still virgins.

In fact, it had been only recently that we'd started holding hands.

I already had a plan for this trip—I wanted us to share our first kiss, at least.

I planned to have a campfire out by the beach, and share our first kiss beneath the stars.

I slipped out of our chambers, and found a lower-level mage, with whom I communicated this intent to. She blushed, nodding and grinning at the idea of being able to help set up such a romantic moment.

I had a picnic basket set up, and taken to the beach. There was wood gathered for a small fire, and everything was ready.

I made my way back to Marielle, and I told her that I had a surprise for her.

I led her out to the beach, and we laughed and played in the surf before finding our way to our picnic, eating some sandwiches and cookies and enjoying the view by the fire.

I glanced over at her.

"Marielle," I murmured, and she looked at me with a blush darkening her cheeks.

"...You've never used that tone before..."

I smiled. "I haven't," I agreed. I leaned in to her. "I've spent the last year getting to know you, and we've been travelling together and growing closer...Marielle, I would like...to take our relationship to a new level. Can we?"

Her blush darkened, and just as she nodded and started to lean in to me...a blast of thunder roiled over us, and rain seemed to dump on us.

She squealed, and we rushed to run toward the tower, laughing as we got pelted by the rain.

"Talk about bad timing!" I huffed as we got beneath a nearby gazebo, and we met eyes.

I could see her perky, small breasts through her blouse, and I felt my face heat up as my heart raced.

She caught my gaze, and our eyes locked...

I leaned forward slowly, wrapping my arm around her waist, and dipped my head toward hers.

She leaned up, meeting me the rest of the way, and our lips met in a flurry of movement and sucking and vulgar slurping noises.

Our tongues met, our teeth nicked each other's, but we didn't care.

I lowered her down to the floor of the gazebo, and it didn't even matter that we were outside, that thunder raged around us, or that the rain sprayed us.

It didn't matter that anyone could see us.

All that mattered was having her.

I gasped as her teeth caught my lip, and I pulled away, moving to nibble on her ear, and she cried out.

I kissed my way down her neck and chest, nibbling her nipples through her top, moving down her torso and pulling up her skirt to move between her legs.

She sobbed in what sounded like anguished pleasure as I kissed her soft, delicate lips.

I spread them, minding the short, trimmed hair, and strove my tongue again and again over the little bead there, as father had told me when I'd hit puberty.

He'd told us boys that it was very important to please a woman—that pleasing her led to the greatest heights, and that if she was pleased, you would be too.

I moved my face in a circle, using my chin to run over her seam even as my tongue swirled her clit, and she gasped and clung her hands in my hair, begging me to help her.

She may not know what was coming, but I did.

I gently inserted a finger into her body, and curled it upward toward the front of her body, and she seized for a moment.

I could feel her walls clamping my finger, a warm thickness excreting out of her innermost self, and then the fluttering pulses as she cried and thrashed.

I looked up at her, admiring her orgasm face, and I felt my dick harden as I watched her cum on my hand and face.

I crawled up her body, and got between her legs, a hand springing my cock free of binding.

"Can I?" I asked. "Can I have you?"

"Yes!" She sobbed. "Just-just give it to me already, please," she pleaded.

I sank into her warm wetness, and I groaned as I pushed through the tiny amount of resistance there.

She gasped, sucking in a sharp breath before she coughed out, cringing, but I gently kept going.

I took my time with her that evening, and by the time I was releasing my cum into her body, the storm clouds were breaking and the stars of the early night were peeking through the sky.

Bonus Chapter 3 — Kadi Jakard Ali

November, 167 Imperial Year

"They are stunning," I gushed over the newest addition to my eldest brother's growing little family, my betrothed at my side and our middle brother across from us, his own family with him.

Kaleem had twin sons and a new daughter.

Cavell had a daughter, and a son on the way.

I was getting married in a few hours, to my betrothed since infancy.

That was why my middle brother had made the journey overseas to come back home and join us for the celebrations.

I was finally sixteen, and so, I had reached marriageable age. Now, it was time to make good on the promise that had been made.

Amir's youngest son, Amin Ali, was a spitting image of his father, according to mother.

Amir had once been one of the prized studs of the palace, and was still quite a looker, despite his age. His sons were all very handsome, and his daughter was beautiful.

The only child whom didn't look like him was the one whom he had adopted, who had originally been born of a concubine and the counterfeit sultan years ago.

He had been raised as a great warrior, who had learned the truth of his identity and had been so ashamed that he had been born of such bad origin, but it made him appreciate his new family all the more.

Amir and his wife were amazing to him, and to their other children.

Amin was a year older than I was, and he was incredibly warm and kind, as well as powerful.

Father and mother were very pleased with him as a prospective groom for me.

He had always been very respectful and courteous with me.

Since I was the princess, and I was marrying a duke, the wedding was originally going to be large…

Amin and I had both opted out for a small, intimate ceremony and banquet, however, wishing to make our way to our new home in quiet peace, and consummate our wedding in our own home.

The wedding arrived a few hours later, and we made our vows.

We got into a carriage and made our way the short journey to our new home.

When we had entered the estate and set away the servants for the night, he and I sat awkwardly on the end of the bed for a while, just sitting in silence.

I glanced at him, and he cleared his throat, meeting my gaze.

"So…" I whispered.

"I...I'm sorry, this is awkward, isn't it?" He asked. "I wanted to take our time, and make you feel good slowly, and have our night...but I admit, I am more nervous than I had—"

I pressed a kiss to his lips—our first kiss.

He sucked in a breath through his nose, and slowly, ever so slowly, relaxed beneath my touch.

He opened his lips when I pressed against them with my tongue, and I moaned when our tongues met.

That night, I took the initiative, and I pulled his hands to my body.

He begged and pleaded with me to forgive him, to have mercy for touching me this way, but I kissed him and told him that I liked his hands on me...and I felt his length throb beneath my place on his lap.

He gasped and punched his hips up when I finally brought myself down onto his naked body, and he cried out in pleasure as I ground my hips and thrust myself onto him.

It didn't last long...maybe ten minutes, but the sounds we made together and the feeling of our joining were euphoric.

He was my closest friend, who had been at my side through my whole life, and I loved him.

January, 169 IY

"She is beautiful," my mother said, rocking my daughter in her arms. "Have you decided on a name for her yet, Kadi?"

I smiled. "Kaia," I said, and my mother gaped at me.

"What…?"

I smiled wider, and Amin took my hand in his.

"We wanted to honor my sister-in-law," he told her.

"I…thank you, Kadi, thank you Amin…" mother said, tearing up and beaming a smile down to my newborn.

She was only days old, and I was sore, but she was beautiful.

She had my silvery-white hair, and her father's bright, vivid golden eyes.

"Kaia," I murmured. "My beautiful baby Kaia."

"Is the trip scheduled?" Amin asked my father, and my father grinned and nodded.

"Yes, we are scheduled to leave next month for our trip to the Western Empire. Cavell and Marielle are going to be inheriting the duchy soon, and Marielle's elder brother will be ascending the throne soon and becoming emperor."

Things were moving forward, time was flowing on, and progress was happening all around the world.

A new world, a new age, was forming. Soon, things would be drastically different.

It was no longer the age of Kynareth, Winter, Cinder and Seryn.

It was no longer the age of Johannes, Karmindy and Dieter.

It was not the age of the dragons and wyverns, or Tyrannical Emperor Kai and Nieves.

No longer was it the era of the Seers, with Carlisle and Kinley.

It was no longer the age of the Seal, with the Conquering Empress, Katariah and her group of consorts.

Soon, it would no longer be the age of Sultans, Sultanas or Abandoned Princes, like my father.

Progress was coming…and the world needed to get ready, for my visions told me that it was going to happen faster than anyone anticipated.

Extras: Name pronunciations and descriptions:

(ALL images used were referenced from Google, just a general base I used to reference character appearances, and can be found on Google.)

Klaus- "Kl-oww-ss", rich tan skin, white-silver hair, rich purple eyes, 6', lean muscular

Name: Klaus Malik (Jakard)
Rank: Crowned Prince, Sorcerer, Keeper Knight, Prince Consort
Faction: Jakard
Mage Mana superior
(DISCLAIMER: found on Google, these are not my images)

Claudianne- "Claw-dee-ehhn", tan skin, peppery-silver hair, lavender eyes, 5'2", average frame

Name: Claudianne Jasmine Jakard
Rank: Arch-duke's daughter, princess, Crowned Princess princess, Queen
Faction: Jakard
Mage Mana inferior
(DISCLAIMER: found on Google, these are not my images)

—Fin—

We hope you enjoyed The Royal's Saga, Book 6:
The Abandoned Prince
Please join us for the next installment of The Royal's Saga:
Book 7: The Decoy Duchess…

Book Excerpt to follow

Preface – Celine

October, 1024 Imperial Lunar Year

It was getting cold, and I didn't know where I was supposed to go.

I had just turned fourteen years old, but there was no celebration.

My father had been a middle-class baron, and had died of a decaying sickness that had been going across the continent at the time, since he had been travelling, and he had come back in a coffin.

My mother, the baroness, had rapidly declined in her own health, and once she failed to keep up the fief...we had been kicked out by my uncle.

We had migrated with some of the homeless into a large city in the empire, not far from the imperial palace.

We had found an alleyway in the middle of the city, and had bunkered down there outside the back of a bakery, where we could snatch the leftovers and burn loaves from the garbage collection and had a good rain-gutter there to put a clay bowl underneath to collect water and drink from.

My mother, however...had succumbed to death, and I was now all alone, here in this gutter. Forgotten and left with nothing.

No future.

"Where are your parents?" A well-dressed woman asked me, holding out a coat for me. I startled, looking at her in shock and taking her in.

She looked…strikingly like *me*, with her wheat-colored hair and her odd, violet-blue eyes.

Standing a few feet behind her and wearing very extravagant clothing, was a teenage boy who had light brown hair and walnut-colored eyes with a slightly golden-hue in the sunset's glowing light. A man who looked much like him stood behind him, and they looked like a father and son.

Right behind him stood a teenage boy with dark, chocolate-colored hair and grayish-green eyes, a medium-muscular build. Nearby stood a man in a butler's suit.

They all sat there staring at me, waiting for a response.

I glanced down the alleyway, toward where my mother's corpse lay, being feasted on by the rats.

The butler stepped up beside of the nobleman from the carriage and nodded, striding down into the alley to take a look where I had been looking.

"Oh, *heavens!*" I heard the sharp cry, and I cringed.

He rushed back out, a handkerchief covering his mouth and nose, his face pale and drained of blood. He shook his head. "There is a woman's *dead body* back there…" The group of nobles stood there, gawking at me. "Girl," the man began. "Is that…woman back there…your mother?"

Tears filled my eyes, but I nodded. "Mmhmm."

"What happened to your father?" The noblewoman asked, her face fearful.

"My father passed away eight years ago," I informed.

They looked at me. "...Was he a nobleman?" The young dark-haired boy asked.

I nodded. "He was a baron. He died of a disease while travelling."

They glanced at one another, and the woman stood as they went and whispered amongst themselves.

Then, the woman came back to me, leaning down to study my face. "And you've been out here on the streets how long?"

I looked to the ground. "...for two years."

"Goodness," she gaped at me. "...How old are you?"

"...I was fourteen a few days ago."

A smile lit their all of their faces as they glanced at one another again, nodding, before the butler came and kneeled before me while the woman went back to the carriage, climbing in with the assistance of the coachman.

"Young miss, would you like to get off of the street? You could have jewels, fancy dresses, lots of toys, and anything else you could wish for. Would you like to come with us?"

I gaped at the group, before I looked back to the butler. "Could...could I have a warm blanket and food?" I asked, in awe.

They all stared at me in silence, before they nodded.

The nobleman looked at me. "Of course," the man said, voice void of emotion.

"You could even have a warm bath," the butler said, smiling at me. "Come, won't you let us take you in?"

I gasped, startled. "You...want to *adopt* me?"

The nobleman gaped, a look of vague disgust and mild horror on his face, before he shook his head. "It is more of a...*business transaction*. You need not worry; you won't be harmed. We will take care of you. There is no need to be concerned."

"But...why? I have nothing...nothing to offer in return. Why me?"

They glanced at one another, but the butler answered me. "You will get an answer to that question soon, if you come with us. You don't have to worry about getting hurt," he told me. "We will take good care of you, and we will send someone over to..." He paled, glancing down the alley again. "We'll prepare a funeral for *her*," he said quickly. "We will be sure that she is cared for."

If I could be taken care of, and they would honor my mother by giving her a proper burial, then I would accept this deal. So, I took the butler's hand as they led me away, to a new life.

I didn't know it at that moment, but that moment would become the catalyst that would change my life forever.

I couldn't fathom all of the things that were about to happen to me, or why, but I was just thankful to be offered the chance to get off of the streets.

Looking back...it would be one of my greatest mistakes. At least, I would think so for a long time.

...
.....
....

....
....
....
....
....
....
....
....
.... **Want to keep reading?**

Be sure keep an eye out for the release of
The Royal's Saga, Book 7: The Decoy Duchess
Release Date set for May, 20, 2023!
Check me out on my social media for updates, extras, and so on!
Handles in the "About the Author" section.

It only gets better from here, and let us not forget: STEAMIER.
...Y
U...
...M!

Books by Kristen Elizabeth

The Royal's Saga

The Apathetic Knight, Part 1
The Apathetic Knight, Part 2
The Villainous Princess
The Disregarded Dragon
The Hidden Queen
The Conquering Empress
The Abandoned Prince
The Decoy Duchess
The Empathetic Brother
The Anonymous Writer
The Luxurious Slave
The Royal's Behind the Scenes Finale Novella

The Shifter's Saga

The Rejected Lady Book 1: Parts 1 & 2
The Rejected Lady Book 2: Parts 3 & 4
The Hunted Cat
The Damned Wolf Parts 1 & 2
The Justified Siren
The Lost Heirs Parts 1 & 2
The Trapped Son
The Shifter's Behind the Scenes Finale Novella

The Lover's Saga

Titles coming soon!

The Spell-Caster's Saga

Titles coming soon!

The Dreamer's Saga

Titles coming soon!

The Queen's Saga

Titles coming soon!

The Knight's Saga

Titles coming soon!

The Immortal's Saga

Titles coming soon!

The Villain's Saga

Titles coming soon!

The Children's Saga (PG13)

Titles coming soon!

Acknowledgments

A special thanks to my proof reader, Trisha, for reading through the novels and helping me with the grammatical and spelling aspects. Without your help, there were a lot of mistakes that would have made it into the books.

A special thanks to those who supported my work, including but not limited to Trisha, Sammie-Anne, Shannon, Amber, and so on. Several people who really encouraged me to write, publish and seek higher things. You guys inspired me to make this possible. I appreciate it so much. Special thanks go to my most avid of fans, including Christine, Jeanna, and a few others who had been following my work and have gone to extra measures above and beyond to support and read my works. All of you aforementioned people make writing the books so much more exciting so that I can see your reactions and give you good books to read! Thank you all for being amazing. Without you, there is no way I would have gotten such a great start!

A special thanks to my husband, Reece, for allowing me to take so much time to write and keeping everything running yourself. You knew how important it was to me to be able to write and complete my works, and you didn't get angry about it. You were always understanding and pushing me to publish the work. You wanted me to pursue my goals, and I needed that extra push because I'm bad about procrastinating on things. I love you, handsome ;)

Lastly, I want to give a special thanks to my mom. You don't even read my work, but you encourage my writing and creativity even if you might not agree with the content. Thank you, and I love you.

About the Author

Kristen Elizabeth is now on social media! Follow on Instagram and Tiktok! Handle for both apps is (lovelymadness92) Follow for more bonus content, updates, and publishing schedules!

Kristen is a stay-at-home mother to two special-needs boys and wife from North Carolina who comes from the rural country, and grew up in a broken home. The daughter of a single mom who tried her best and worked multiple jobs to keep a roof over their heads.

Kristen spent the majority of her life emersed in arts and music, and used writing and reading as an opportunity to escape from the trauma and depression that spiraled out of control from the abusive background she crawled out of.

Writing, arts and music opened up an entirely new world for her, and she kept herself surrounded by it to avoid the stress and anxiety that was forcing down on her.

Kristen, herself, is also on the Autism Spectrum, and wants to share her unique worlds with those around her. She doesn't think she's all that special, but hopefully, someone out there will enjoy her creations as much as she does and use her creations to escape from the mundane everyday life.

Kristen's biggest goal is to fit somewhere outside of the norm, and to broaden horizons in the world of fiction.

Life isn't always happy endings, sunshine, and rainbows.

Sometimes, life is an utter freakshow and things don't work out the way you hoped.

That's something that Kristen wants to bring to her writing.

None of this happens without the readers and fans, and any and all sharing and spreading the word means so much to me!

Thank you to all of my dear readers,

Kristen Elizabeth

Made in the USA
Columbia, SC
21 May 2023